CU20847151

MILLER'S END

KEITH FINNEY

Keith Finney - Author

INTRODUCTION

An Invitation

Welcome to your invitation to join my Readers' Club.

Receive free, exclusive content only available to members—including short stories, character interviews and much more.

To join, click on the link towards the end of this book and you're in!

1

ELECTRIC WIND

A brisk February morning on England's East Coast called for a sturdy constitution, paper tissues, and well-insulated walking boots. At least that was what Anthony Stanton, or Lord Stanton, as he was more formally addressed, thought necessary.

He could tell from Lyn Blackmore's look of pity that she did not share his assessment of winter on the Norfolk Broads.

"I wouldn't mind, Ant, but you're an army man. How on earth did you manage on deployment?"

Ant inspected the drip of liquid he had just removed from the tip of his nose with a gloved hand, before turning his back on the prevailing wind blowing off the North Sea.

"I didn't find much need for thermal underwear or earmuffs in the Middle East, Lyn. Anyway, you should talk. That coat and fluffy hat make you look like a Turkish rug gone walkabout."

Lyn bridled while smoothing her llama-wool ensemble with a hand-encased mitten. "I'll have you know this is the latest fashion. You are a philistine sometimes." She gave a twirl to emphasise her point, a corner of the long garment flicking up as a gust of wind caught hold.

Ant smiled as he caught a glimpse of her brightly coloured leggings decorated with polar bears wearing sunglasses and holding what looked like piña coladas. "And somewhere on the Yorkshire Moors, there's a load of the beasties shivering, just so you can stay nice and toasty."

Ant jabbed a finger at Lyn's coat, its wispy down swaying back and forth against each new gust of icy wind.

Lyn gave her hat a tug to ensure it completely covered her ears. "I think you will find the collective noun for a gathering of llamas is a cria herd. Also, the wool is sustainably harvested on regulated farms, so there."

Ant frowned. "Never heard anything so daft in all my life. I know you head teachers. If you don't know the answer to something, you just make it up."

Lyn laughed as she wiped a wind-induced tear from her eye. "That's as maybe, but on this occasion, I am telling you the truth. The term is derived fro—"

Ant held up his hands in mock surrender. "Enough already, it's too cold for a school lesson. Anyway, don't get me going on that sustainability stuff. Look at that lot."

Turning around to face the full onslaught of the onshore wind bullying its way across the Hemsby coastline, he pointed south-eastward to Scroby Sands wind farm. The triffid-like structures stood only two miles off the coast from Great Yarmouth, though to Ant's eye, it looked like they lined the horizon like steel sentinels fending off strangers from afar.

Lyn glanced over her friend's shoulder.

"And?"

"That lot. Look at them. About as useful as a chocolate

fireguard." Ant extended his arm and pointed an accusing finger.

Lyn had her arms folded. The look of rapprochement was one Ant knew well as he attempted to defend himself.

"What is it they are not doing?"

Lyn tutted. "There you go again with your rubbish diction. If you mean that elegant testimony to modernity and sustainability, which are currently stationary, yes I had noticed."

Ant worked hard not to bite. He knew Lyn often got the better of him and tried in vain not to make his irritation too evident.

"And you say I talk rubbish. Anyway, tell me this. It's cold enough to give every heating system in the kingdom a fit of the screaming abdabs and sufficiently gusty to keep all wearers of toupees indoors with a pot of glue. Yet the very things that are supposed to work quite well in the wind to help keep us warm appear to have withdrawn their labour —go figure?"

Ant continued to chunter as he waved an arm at the stationary objects that he thought had drawn their design inspiration from the *War of the Worlds*.

"Enough of this. Come on, we've got some granny-sitting to do, which is something else you got me roped into without asking beforehand."

Ant gave Lyn a fleeting sideways glance as he passed her on his way back to his beloved Morgan sports car. He chose to ignore her look of pity.

"Don't you put that one on me, Anthony Stanton. You were the one who said we should take an active interest in the community. Anyway, helping Burt Bampton show a group of pensioners around his mill can hardly be described as work, can it? Anyway, if I'd have told you beforehand, you'd have refused, wouldn't you? And will you please slow down; you're kicking sand all over my coat."

Ant half turned. "Not at all, I like Burt. It's just... oh, never mind, let's get on with it. Anyway, I thought llama wool is supposed to be tough as old boots?"

Lyn paused and flicked up the thick collar of her coat against the wind.

"It is, except it cost me a lot more than a pair of old boots, silly."

———

TWENTY MINUTES later found the Morgan purring up a narrow track boarded by a steep bank to the left and a field drainage ditch on the right. Poking above the grassy bank, the stationary sails of Bampton Mill stood proud, and as the car rounded a bend, the full glory of the ancient brick and wooden structure revealed itself against an angry looking Norfolk sky.

"Look, Lyn, it's Burt. I wouldn't like to be up top on a day like this."

What am I saying? I will be in half an hour.

He turned to Lyn, her expression telling him she knew what he was thinking.

"Give him a wave before the man takes off."

Lyn's instruction drew Ant's attention back to the mill. On the top level and resting against a thin wooden rail, Burt hung on for all he was worth as he braced against the chilly wind. Nevertheless, the miller wore the broadest smile Ant had seen in a long time.

"Morning, Burt," shouted Ant as he attempted to make himself heard against the howling winter blast.

He wasn't sure if Burt had caught his words but guessed he got the gist as the miller waved with his free hand.

Ant and Lyn continued to argue about renewable energy and the sustainability of llama wool until he brought the Morgan to a stop. Twenty feet ahead stood the imposing mill, which stood majestically in its landscape. Only the occasional flapping of wooden siding gave any clue about the weather conditions.

"Can we just agree to disagree, Lyn? You're giving me a headache, and quite frankly, I just want to get out of this stupid wind."

Lyn smiled as she rounded her side of the car and caught hold of Ant's arm, rubbing his coat vigorously as if massaging his circulation back into life.

"I'm happy to talk about something else, Ant, as long as you don't mention the weather again for at least an hour. You really are a big softie."

Ant smiled as he covered Lyn's hand with his own. About to make further comment, his flow was interrupted by Burt bounding out of the mill entrance.

"Morning, you two. Thanks for helping out. There's about a dozen of 'em coming. And they'll be here any minute."

Ant extended an arm to shake Burt's hand.

"You got down pretty damn quick, matey. One of these days you'll do yourself an injury flying up and down those stairs."

Burt laughed as he turned to Lyn, giving her an energetic hug seemingly designed to squeeze the life out of her.

"Let go of me, you big galoot. You'll have my eyeballs popping out if you squeeze much harder."

Burt roared, his ample frame jiggling up and down rhythmically.

"Soft lad here wants to get inside, and you know what he's like when he's cold."

Lyn and Burt gave Ant a look somewhat like a clown pulling a sad face.

Ant sniffed and cleared his throat in protest. He looked longingly at the gnarled wooden door to the mill as it pivoted lazily in the wind, its sheer weight mounting an effective defence against the gale.

"Hope you're ready for the onslaught. I think I've got everything prepared for them," said Burt.

Just then the sound of a vehicle horn floated on the wind, its intensity rising and falling in concert with the prevailing conditions.

"Speak of the devil. Bang on time too. I thought I'd say a few words out here first, then move them all inside."

Ant pulled a face. Having glimpsed the cozy interior of the mill, he felt as if he'd been forced to give his last remaining pear drop away.

Will we ever get out of this stupid wind?

A battered minivan pulled up next to Ant's Morgan. Inside, several of the occupants pressed their faces against the grimy glass, straining to get a glimpse of the welcoming party.

"That thing has seen better days."

Burt wasn't addressing his comments to anyone in particular.

"You can say that again," replied Lyn. "How the heck did that make it all the way here from Walsingham?"

Ant half turned, looking at Lyn through eyes almost closed as a defence against the swirling dust, which he'd noticed seemed to permanently encase the old mill.

"What do you mean? It's only thirty miles away, Lyn."

She raised both eyebrows and smiled.

"Exactly my point."

Before there was an opportunity for further discussion, the rickety doors of the minivan slid open. Eventually, it's elderly occupants variously stumbled, limped, and groaned the eighteen inches from the van's interior onto the weather-beaten earth.

Ant leant over to whisper in Burt's ear.

"Now I understand, you old goat. We're here as care workers, not guides. How in heaven's name do you intend to get that lot up top?" To emphasise his point, Ant pulled back and pointed to the wood-tiled apex of the imposing mill, its large wooden sails tied back to the structure with heavy hessian rope.

Burt smiled. The glint in the miller's eye left Ant with no doubt the morning was going to be a challenging one.

"Good morning, everyone."

Ant glanced at the visitors and realised few had heard Burt's words.

"Best get leeward of the mill, Burt, or you'll never make yourself heard." He pointed to his right.

The mill owner nodded, gave Ant the thumbs up, and gestured for the small gathering to follow him.

The change in body language was immediate. Shoulders dropped, eyes were dabbed, and collars lowered as all felt the instant relief from the biting wind.

"Goodness, that's better, yes?"

Heads nodded, and smiles abounded as the group huddled as near to the mill as they could comfortably gather. The cruel wind was unable to get at them as the structure's cone-like shape made the onslaught take a forced detour around the group.

"Right, now we can get going," began Burt. "But first I

would like to formally welcome the Windy Wanderers to Bampton Mill."

Ant and Lyn looked at each other, trying to stifle a child-like snigger.

"Tell you what, Lyn. If this lot are anything like Pops' little problem, it won't be the reference to 'wind' in the group's name we should be worried about." He bumped her shoulder with his as they leant into each other conspiratorially.

Lyn's shoulders heaved as Ant's words sank in.

"I seem to remember he always blamed Gideon."

Ant nodded, smiling broadly at the memory of a much-missed grandfather and his faithful Labrador.

Suddenly Ant realised the talking had stopped; everyone was looking at him. Embarrassed, he gave Lyn a sideways glance before clearing his throat. Ant looked at Burt intensely as if taking keen interest in events and prayed someone would give him a clue as to what was going on.

"As I was saying," said Burt, grinning broadly at the two miscreants. "I am pleased to tell you that we have a real-life member of the English nobility with us."

Ant groaned inwardly and glanced at Lyn, who was enjoying the moment rather too much for his liking.

Here we go.

"Ant never tires of telling anyone who'll listen that his family has lived at Stanton Hall since 1667, won on the turn of a card, would you believe. And with the estate came the title: Earl of Stanton. Do you want to explain the rest, Ant?"

Burt smiled broadly as Ant's cheeks reddened.

Your turn will come, old friend.

"No, no," Ant replied, attempting to give off a superior air and failing spectacularly as his nose began to drip. "You are doing such a fine job that I shall leave it to you."

Ant's embarrassment wasn't helped by the sound of Lyn chuckling loud enough for all to hear.

Burt accepted Ant's invitation to continue.

"Today the title Earl of Stanton is held by his father, which means our friend with the drippy nose receives the courtesy title of Lord Stanton."

The announcement was met with a collective "oooh" as several heads turned in Ant's direction.

It's like living in a flaming zoo.

Burt wasn't finished as he provided even more detail.

"And to confuse things even further, ladies and gentlemen, Ant's actual family name isn't 'Stanton.' It is Norton-D'Arcy. This makes his father's full title, 'Sir Gerald Norton-D'Arcy, Fifth Earl of Stanton,' and Ant's, 'Lord Anthony Norton-D'Arcy of Stanton.' Everybody clear?"

Ant shook his head and attempted to make himself disappear into his oversized coat.

"Well, I don't approve of gambling," offered a voice from the back of the group. No one owned up to the contribution. Herd instinct took over as a collective giggle began. Tension broken, Ant popped his head from within his coat like a tortoise launching forth from its shell to grab a piece of lettuce.

"Come on, let's get you all inside and swap Ant's family's gambling problem for the fascinating history of my mill."

The group needed no further encouragement to escape the harsh conditions and shuffled through the narrow door like eager shoppers trying to buy the last cup of coffee in existence.

"Not so quick, you lot."

Lyn's order brought matters to a sudden halt. Her best head-teacher voice had done the trick.

"I'm sure you would like a group photo for your newsletter, or whatever you have, to mark your visit to this historic mill? Lyn held her iPhone up so that no one could be in any doubt about her intentions. "Come on, get in a huddle in front of the door. If I stand back far enough, I can get you all in plus a good bit of the mill."

Ant scowled. Lyn's command had left them standing in a force-ten gale now they had left the relative calm of the sheltered side of the mill. All he wanted to do was to blend into the background for the next hour or so.

Instead, all Lyn wanted to do was humiliate Ant further by having him photographed. He could just see *The Clarion* local free paper's headline: "Windy Wanderers Have Blowout at Mill on Hill."

"Right, everyone, say cheese," shouted Lyn as she lined up the shot on the screen of her phone.

Cheese? I can think of one or two choicer words.

"Well done, I think I got you all in, and a great police mugshot it will make too."

Ant wagged a finger at Lyn to indicate it was bad form to laugh at your own jokes. Judging by the half-smiles of the pink-cheeked assembly, he was clear all they wanted to do was get out of the wind.

A COMMUNAL SIGH permeated the cozy interior of the mill's ground floor as Ant shut the entrance door, and with it banished the appalling weather. It had been some time since he'd visited the mill and had forgotten just how atmospheric it was.

"Right, everyone. Now we're out of that silly weather, I—"

"Mr Bampton, I think you mean, gale?"

The miller let out a roar.

"Nowt but a bit rafty as we say around these parts. It's Mr Sidcup, isn't it? I tell you what: I'll call you Albert if you call me Burt."

The man, who stood at least nine inches taller than anyone else in the room, displayed a sour face.

"That will not be necessary, Mr Bampton. And I know what rafty means. I am, after all, from, as you put it, round here."

An awkward stillness descended as Albert's cold response permeated the intimate space. No one moved. Then Ant noticed a petite woman standing next to the man. She was tugging gently on his arm while wearing a broad smile.

"Albert, don't be so stuffy. Burt's only trying to make us feel welcome."

Susan Mylnweard's intervention did the trick. Albert's shoulders dropped; his facial expression softened.

"I apologise, Burt."

"Nothing to apologise for, my friend."

Ant leant into Lyn. "I wonder whether those two are together?"

Lyn shrugged her shoulders. "Dunno, but she's certainly got the measure of him."

"Come on, Burt, get on with it. It'll be summer before we've finished if you're not careful."

Ant's attempt to break the ice by putting the focus back on Burt worked a treat. The miller immediately picked up on his friend's cue by offering his visitors refreshments.

"The grain dust will soon get to you, folks, so I suggest you grab a drink. Sorry, it's only barley cordial, but believe me, it's the best thing to keep your throat lubricated."

"You mean except for Fen Bodger pale ale, Burt."

"Lordy, Ant. You mean you still drink that stuff?"

Ant laughed. Everyone else, except Lyn, looked on in mild bemusement.

"Better than that fizzy lemonade stuff you call lager, mate."

Lyn frowned. "Enough, you two, this is a mill tour not a pub crawl."

"More's the pity," offered the faceless voice that had made the earlier quip.

Fed up of waiting, twelve shivering seniors moved towards a timber trestle table on which rested sufficient cordial-filled paper cups to quench an army. Three large plates of assorted biscuits completed the welcome offering. Moving in unison, they forced Ant into a corner of the mill, effectively sandwiching him between the edge of the trestle table, Burt, and an old potbelly stove.

"Good job you didn't light it," whispered Ant as he was pressed tight against the mill owner by the surging horde.

Burt struggled to turn sufficiently to see Ant's face. "Too right. I nearly did but ran out of time."

"You've no idea how pleased I am about that," replied Ant as he strained to pull his midriff from the stove by placing an open palm on the top plate to brace himself.

Rather than the crush abating, as one Windy Wanderer grabbed a soft drink and a biscuit or two, they were replaced by the next eager visitor.

It's like a whirlpool.

Burt brought Ant back from his wanderings as he handed him one of the flimsy cups. "Here, grab this while there's any left." The miller half lifted his right arm as he struggled against the throng pressing against him. "Oops, sorry mate."

Ant grabbed the drink, shaking his head to indicate the

spots of spilled liquid on his shoulder were of no consequence.

"Have you got yours?"

Burt nodded towards the table. "Yep, that's mine on the corner. That's if no one nicks it before I can get to it."

The two men swapped weary grins.

"So how much is the mill worth, then?"

At first, Ant thought the man pressing into his right side was talking to him. About to ask what he meant, he realised the question was aimed at Burt. However, his friend was too busy attempting to open a space between himself and a slightly built woman to his front to notice.

"I think he's talking to you, Burt."

Even though Ant stood over six foot in his stockinged feet, he had to twist his neck to catch the inquisitor's eye. He realised the miller didn't stand a chance of freeing himself sufficiently to engage the man while protecting the lady from being squashed, so he acted.

"Everyone, step back, please, or someone will get hurt."

2

STAIRWAY TO HEAVEN

T he room fell silent as Ant's authoritative voice filled the space. He caught Lyn smiling at the rear of the group. She held her paper cup up as if proposing a toast to him.

This is going to get worse before it gets better.

He grimaced as the group inexplicably moved forward before retreating and melting into a loose huddle.

Ant sensed Burt falling and instinctively eased forward to steady his friend. From the corner of his eye, he noticed the miller's drink about to tip from the table. Without thinking, he stretched and caught it just in time.

"Good catch," observed a woman to Ant's left.

He grinned at the elderly lady, whose contented smile and twinkling eyes reminded him of a much-missed great-aunt from his childhood.

"Cricket was the only team-thing I got into at school," replied Ant as he winked at the friendly face.

Keen to engage his new friend in conversation, Ant's attempt was cut short by the now-familiar tone.

"You haven't answered my question."

All eyes fell on the man. Several Windy Wanderers groaned, which gave Ant an indication in what regard the group held the rude man.

Before Burt had a chance to gather his thoughts, the slim lady who he'd been trying to protect from the crush, spoke.

"There you go again; don't be such a bore. You know, I wish you could hear yourself sometimes." The woman curled a hand around the tall man's arm and gave it a squeeze.

That's the second time she's pulled him back into line; they must be an item.

"Hi, I'm Susan, and this big lump is... well, you may remember from earlier that his name is Albert. Don't worry, his bark is much worse than his bite."

Ant watched the man blush as Susan gave his arm another squeeze.

Yep, they had something going even if he is as daft as a box of frogs.

Burt took his opportunity.

"That's okay, er, Susan. Well, Albert, just let me say it's worth more today than when my forebears acquired the mill. As for its current value, well, as my grandmother used to say, 'money and fair words.' Neither inviting nor waiting for a response, Burt continued, "Now, ladies and gentlemen, again, welcome to Bampton Mill. I'm guessing from your club name that you have visited many such buildings, so can I just remind everyone how dangerous these old places can be."

Ant noted the attention everyone, including Albert, though still sulking, paid to Burt's words.

"The steps to all floors are incredibly steep, narrow, and pass through low bulkheads, so watch your heads. Unfortunately, it will not be possible to demonstrate the mill in operation today because of the high winds. Nevertheless, the machinery is still dangerous, so please take care not to bump into anything harder than you."

"Doesn't mean you, Ken, since your head's empty," mumbled the group heckler making his third intervention. Ken shook his head and smiled.

Burt led a chorus of chuckles as he began to move off.

"Okay, follow me, and remember, please watch your heads."

Ant squeezed through the group to reach Lyn.

"Hello, stranger."

"Hello, you."

As Burt began climbing the narrow stairs, Ant became aware of heated whispers between two elderly ladies who had managed to separate themselves from the rest of the group. He looked at Lyn.

"I know, identical twins," she said in a quiet tone.

Blimey.

As the tussle continued, both worked their way through the thinning crowd as more of Burt's visitors ascended the stairs.

"Now, ladies. What's all this about? If you don't want to go up, it's fine. I'll stay with you and tell you a bit about the mill's history."

Ant's amusement grew, knowing Lyn's attempt to calm tempers had failed miserably. She was about to find that blood really was thicker than water.

"Not at all. We're not invalids, you know," said one of the women. The other nodded her agreement.

Ant tried to intervene. "I don't think Lyn was—"

"It's all her fault," said one woman, pointing to the other. "She spilt a jar of pickled gherkins all over my hiking trousers just before we came out this morning. The only other thing I had to hand was this."

The elderly lady gripped the seam of her flowing dress with each hand. She pulled sideways, which separated the pleats until the dress took on a triangular shape. "And just look at those steps. If I go up there, I'll be showing my drawers to the whole of Norfolk."

Lyn tried again to calm tempers. "Sorry, I didn't catch your names?"

The two women glared at each other before turning to Lyn in unison.

"I'm Petal, and this is my older sister, Daisy. She's the clumsy one."

Ant matched Lyn's look of surprise.

"Oh, I thought you were identical sisters for a moment."

The two women once more scowled at each another.

"We are, but she was born six minutes before me, so she thinks she the oldest sister and can boss me about."

Daisy raised an eyebrow. "Never mind her, she's always had a chip on her shoulder, silly woman. As if it was my fault I arrived first. Still, at least it proves I can make decisions. She can't make her mind up about anything, ever."

Before Petal could reply, Ant attempted to change the subject.

"What lovely names. They have a ring to them, don't they?"

Ant soon realised he'd mirrored Lyn's earlier error of judgement as the sisters resumed their bickering.

"Mother was a botanist. Apparently, she thought giving us these stupid names would be fun because we were born in mid-summer, just before those silly plants flower. We hate them."

Daisy's words met with the full approval of Petal.

Lyn seized her opportunity. "Well, at least you agree on something. Now let's get you upstairs. Ant will lead, and I shall bring up the rear, so to speak."

Ant choked back a snigger as he conjured up a mental image he'd rather forget.

"Better you than me, Lyn."

She raised an eyebrow and tilted her head in the direction of the mill steps while whispering to Ant. "Don't say another word, or I'll change my mind and leave you to view a pair of bloomers Queen Victoria would have been proud to call her own."

Ant needed no further incentive and made for the bottom of the steps.

He soon heard a succession of howls from above as first one, then another, made a variety of noises as they hit their foreheads on the low bulkhead. Deciding not to state the obvious, Ant waited for the last of the visitors to clear the steps before joining them as they huddled around Burt.

"I can see from the number of men rubbing their heads that you fell foul of what has become known in these parts as 'the headhunter.'" Burt pointed at the timber joist which formed the bulkhead, so creating the gap in the floor that allowed the steps to pass through it. "Don't worry, I can't see any blood. More importantly, no damage done to my paintwork."

Ant guessed Burt's joke was one of several he regularly trotted out during mill tours.

Don't give up the day job.

Burt wasn't finished. "At least you all have a fine head of hair to protect your skulls, so that's lucky, except for this gentleman." Burt was pointing to a man in the middle of the group.

Ant looked puzzled hearing all but one of the Windy

Wanderers laugh until he realised the silent one had the longest comb-over he'd ever seen.

Amazing how far you can make a dozen strands of hair go.

"He's only joking, Ron," floated a voice from the rear of the group.

Ronald Busby's face remained as cold as stone as he made a point of rearranging his comb-over, eyes firmly fixed on Burt.

Ant decided to take over.

This could get serious.

"I wonder if I might explain how the mill works, Burt?" He winked at his nervous-looking friend. "Let's see if I can remember what you taught me."

Ant spent ten minutes running through the process of grinding grain into flour, pointing out the purpose each floor of the mill fulfilled. His intervention did the trick as attention soon waned from Ron. Instead, eyes darted from one bit of kit to another as Ant continued his exposition.

"And finally, at least for now ladies and gentlemen, let me just say from here on in, you are free to explore the mill at your leisure. Burt will be on the decking surrounding the top floor. Lyn and I will take floors two and three respectively, so you are kept safe. However, can I just state the obvious that if you do go out onto the decking, please be careful. We don't want anyone taking off in this wind. We failed to find the last one!"

Ant's joke met with greater success than Burt's earlier attempt. As the group fragmented, the majority wearing broad smiles, Burt passed Ant as he made his way to the top floor.

"Thanks, mate. I made a bit of a mess of that."

Ant nudged his friend as he passed by.

"No sweat, Burt. Thanks to the briefing note you sent me the other day—I just about got away with it."

Both men smiled. Ant noticed Lyn wagging a finger at him.

"You're a lucky devil. One of these days that smile of yours won't get you out of trouble. Still, I'm impressed you bothered to read Burt's notes."

Ant offered Lyn a slight bow. "I'll take that as a compliment then, shall I?"

Lyn placed a hand on each hip. "Well, at least it proves you can read, I suppose. I can't remember the last time I saw a book in your hands."

Ant drew in his chest and mirrored Lyn's hand-on-hip stance.

"Man of action—me. No time for book theory."

Unable to hold his breath, he had no option but to let his chest fall, causing a small portion of his stomach to over-spill his trouser waist. He could see Lyn pointing to the offending site.

"Oh, really?"

Before Ant could respond, his attention was drawn to Albert cornering Burt at the foot of the steps, which gave access to the second floor.

"Have you ever thought of selling the place?"

The man's voice seemed to Ant to have a sharp edge.

Burt shook his head, half pushed past the tall man and grabbed for a rickety handrail.

"Look, the mill has been in my family for generations. If I have anything to do with it, that will remain the case into the future. I have no wish to be impolite, but we do need to get on."

Ant thought about intervening again but considered the

matter closed as Burt turned from Albert and launched himself up the steep steps two at a time.

That bloke is a pain.

Lyn crossed the grain-dusted floor and rested a reassuring hand on his arm.

"Let's keep 'em moving. You blind 'em with science; I'll play the impatient head teacher."

Ant returned Lyn's reassuring smile.

You always seem to know what to do.

Suddenly there was a chorus of screams from the upper floors.

Ant leapt up two flights of stairs quicker than he had ever moved before. On the top floor, he watched several members of the Windy Wanderers recoiling in horror. He followed their gaze to an open door that led out to the decking which Burt had been making for. Racing past the group, he made for the outside. A brutal wind permeated the mill as he gripped the door frame to steady himself as he took in the scene unfolding outside.

Burt was struggling to hang on to a broken handrail, which was the only thing keeping him from plunging forty feet to the ground and certain death.

"Help me! He's crazy. Get him away from me!"

Burt's anguished cry made Ant loom to his left. On the timber decking sat Ron Busby, his back resting against the timber sidings of the mill, his feet stretched out before him as if he was having a leisurely rest.

"I tripped over the threshold and fell forward into the miller. I meant him no harm; it was an accident. All this fuss over nothing."

Ant noticed the man wore an air of someone who had been unjustly accused of something for which he was completely innocent.

Why is he sitting there instead of helping Burt? Doesn't make sense.

In a split second, Ant had grabbed Burt and pulled the shaken man back to safety. As Burt let go of the handrail, it finally gave way and plummeted to the ground, making a sickening thump which could be heard over the surging wind.

"Let's get you sorted, fella." Ant put a shoulder under one of Burt's arms, grabbed his wrist, and helped him into the mill. "He's okay, everyone: just a bit shook up, that's all."

Several worried faces stared back at the two men. A chorus of voices offered good wishes and repeated suggestions of sweet tea as a remedy for shock. Ant looked around the small room, its timber walls sloping sharply inwards as the building neared its full height. He noticed one absence.

Strange, Albert stayed downstairs.

The hubbub subsided as Burt almost fell into an old elm chair, its spindles creaking as it took his full weight. There was another movement that caught the group's attention. Ron Busby made his way through the doorway and calmly shut the thick wood door behind him. He turned to look at Burt without making any comment while rearranging his comb-over.

"How you doing, Burt?" whispered Ant as he leant over his friend.

Burt nodded. "I'm fine, but let's get this lot downstairs. I think I've had enough for today."

Despite Lyn's protest, Burt insisted on leading the way down.

"Well, that's enough excitement for one day, ladies and gentlemen. Let's get you all back onto terra firma."

A spontaneous round of gentle applause filled the space

as a red-faced Burt acknowledged the group's best wishes. Only Ron Busby failed to join in.

"Now remember what I said; be careful as we go down. The safest way to descend the stairs is to come down backwards, holding on to both handrails and facing the steps. Everyone got it?"

A quiet fell on the group as each person concentrated on Burt's instruction. As the miller made his way to the stair opening, Ron Busby raced over to be next down. As before, Ant and Lyn brought up the rear to make sure everyone made it down safely.

One floor down, Albert Sidcup waited patiently and without comment for his turn to descend the final set of steps to the ground floor. As Ant and Lyn waited with Albert and several other group members to continue their descent, a sickening thud filled the dusty air.

"Oh no, for the love of God."

Ant recognised the voice as belonging to Ron Busby.

"Burt's fallen. I think he's dead."

3

HEADLINES

A momentary hush fell over Bampton Mill as the full implications of Burt's fall sank in. Lyn instinctively guided those around her away from the stairwell and offered what comfort she could. Ant moved quickly to take charge of events.

"Come up, come up now so that I can get to Burt."

Albert Sidcup complied with Ant's instruction in an instant yet couldn't stop looking at the stricken miller as he made his way back up the worn treads of the stairs.

"For goodness' sake, man, keep your eyes on where you are going. There's nothing you can do for Burt at the moment, and the last thing we need is you toppling on top of him."

The sound of such an authoritative order snapped Sidcup out of morbid fixation with the contorted figure on the mill floor. Seconds later he cleared the stairs, leaving free access for Ant to descend. Once safely down, he looked up to see Lyn hot on his trail.

"Careful, Lyn. Here, let me help you avoid poor Burt."

She extended a hand while holding on tight to a

handrail with the other. Ant's careful manoeuvring got Lyn safely off the last step and clear of Burt's crumpled frame.

They stood over their motionless friend, one on either side of his body: waiting, watching, hoping.

"Any sign of a pulse, Ant?"

As Lyn spoke, Ant crouched over Burt's still torso and placed two fingers to the exposed side of the man's neck.

Come on, Burt. Stay with us, mate.

"Yes?"

Ant slowly looked up to meet Lyn's worried gaze. He gave an almost imperceptible shake of his head. It was if he didn't want to acknowledge the truth of what his touch was revealing.

"Damn, damn."

Ant's stifled tone failed to disguise the suppressed anger he felt at losing a good friend.

What a stupid way to die.

He raised his head, eyes closed, whispering a prayer, something he'd promised himself would never happen again after the death of his brother. When he opened them, his field of vision was filled with a neat semicircle of heads looking down on the scene from the stairwell of the first floor.

What are they gawping at?

Ant wanted to vent his anger at the mawkish onlookers. The gentle touch of Lyn's hand on his arm advised him otherwise. He instinctively turned his attention to Lyn and watched as she closed Burt's eyes.

"Sleep well, Burt."

Ant and Lyn exchanged glances as they stood back from Burt's body. A murmur from above distracted his attention from the sad scene.

Better get this lot sorted.

"Lyn, can you ring the emergency services while I get this lot down?" He pointed to the semicircle of heads poking out from the first-floor opening.

Lyn nodded. Half turning, she retrieved her mobile while putting as much space between herself and the stairway so that she could speak in a modicum of privacy.

Meanwhile, Ant asked visitors to make their way down, which proceeded in silence. That was except for the scraping of shoe soles on the dusty steps. Ant took particular care to guide each one of them over Burt's body, which lay immediately at the foot of the stairs, making him difficult to avoid.

"That's it, gently now," said Ant as he successfully delivered everyone to ground level without mishap. Eager to clear the mill, Ant understood why each person, in turn, stood by the side of Burt's body for a few seconds. Some looked bewildered, seemingly not believing what their eyes told them, others wore faces etched with sorrow. Only one, Ron Busby, caught Ant's particular attention. He seemed to linger, give Burt a cold stare, then move off, giving Ant the briefest of unblinking glances.

That's an odd way to react.

"Okay, my friends, nothing to be done at the moment. The police will be here soon, and I'm sure they will wish to speak to each one of you. However, they will also expect the mill to be clear of people. May I suggest, given the weather, that you all make your way to the minibus. I'm sure you'll be called when they want you."

No one answered. Instead, the group began a sombre shuffle to the mill door. When the first to reach it opened the heavy construction, he hesitated as a rush of cold wind filled the mill, causing grain dust to swirl around like a mini tornado.

"It's okay, we have to get you all out of here; it can't be helped." Ant gave the man a reassuring smile. "But please, don't disturb anything as you pass through. The police will not thank us for damaging the crime scene."

A gasp swarmed around the small space as Ant's words sank in. He immediately realised what he'd said.

"Please don't be alarmed. When the police attend a scene such as this, they will automatically treat it as a possible crime scene until they rule out foul play. I meant nothing more than that."

Ant looked towards Lyn, who held her mobile close to one ear and a finger in the other.

"Now, as quietly and quickly as possible, please." He gestured towards the door. Within a minute the mill stood empty apart from Lyn, Ant, and Burt, or at least Ant thought that to be the case. It was only when he turned around to view his friend's twisted corpse that he noticed a woman standing over Burt's lifeless body. Her head bent at the neck as if paying homage to the fallen.

"Such a tragedy," whispered the woman. "I'm sure it will be awful for his poor family."

Her words hit Ant like an electric shock. He looked across to Lyn to see her placing her mobile back into her coat pocket.

"It's Susan, isn't it?" Lyn's words settled on the woman with the gentleness of a feather dancing as it falls. "Don't worry, we'll see to that. Now, let's get you back with the others."

The silence which fell as the door closed behind the last of the Wanderers was disturbed only by the occasional creaking of mill timbers as they resisted an angry easterly.

Ant gazed around the ground floor, finding it difficult to match the ordinariness of the scene with the forlorn shape of Burt as he lay motionless on the stone floor. He wandered over to the small semicircular pine table that Burt seemed to have used for his breaks. He noticed a copy of the *Eastern Daily Press* spread over a mangle of everyday objects. The paper's headline jarred.

"The Good Times Are Back"

He couldn't help but let out a throaty laugh, although humour was the last thing on his mind.

"What's wrong with you?" Lyn's confused look caused Ant to hold up the headline. "Forty-five minutes ago, we were crammed in here like sardines, and Burt was doing his best to stop people being crushed. Now, look at..." Ant's words tailed off as his gaze was drawn back to Burt.

Lyn silently crossed the mill floor until she stood at Ant's side, each looking at their prone friend.

"Makes you think about things, doesn't it?"

Ant nodded as he reached out for her hand. She gave a knowing squeeze.

"I never went to see his body, you know. Couldn't bring myself to do it."

He felt Lyn's eyes on him as he attempted to stem a trickle of tears making their way down his flushed cheeks.

"Come here, let me get rid of those for you." Ant's head dipped as Lyn brushed her cuff against his face, the gentle down of her coat wiping away his tears. "It wasn't your fault, you know. Your brother crashed the car. He was on his own. Who can know what really happened?"

Ant leant into Lyn, who responded by brushing his hand with her own.

"Greg's death, any death, is horrible. But just at this minute, we have to look after Burt, yes?"

Right as usual.

Before Ant could dwell further on the deaths of his brother and friend, the low rumble of a motorbike engine reverberated around the building. Seconds later, the mill door flew open.

"Sorry, didn't mean for it to do that," said a muffled voice.

A figure swathed in black leathers carrying a huge backpack filled the open doorway. Pulling a jet-black crash helmet over their head revealed the wearer to be a young woman.

"Good heavens, Liz?"

Ant's surprised look took his attention momentarily away from Burt as he took in the tiny frame swathed in leathers. He looked at Lyn, who seemed to be having trouble taking it all in.

The briefest of faint smiles crossed the woman's cheeks before being replaced by concern as she concentrated on Burt's crumpled body. She crossed the floor, swung her heavy backpack off so that it rested by her side, and knelt down, her face close to Burt's head.

"Can you hear me?"

She felt for his hand and held it. "Can you hear me?" she repeated, squeezing his hand as she spoke. After checking Burt's airways and feeling for a pulse, she reached for the radio strapped to her shoulder and lifted it away from its harness.

"November Zulu 264. On scene. Ambulance required, blues and twos not needed at this time." The woman gently placed Burt's hand back across his body before pressing the call button on her radio again. "Patient recorded as deceased at 13.22 hours. Out."

Relocating her radio in its shoulder harness, the woman looked at the steep stairway, then back at Burt before turning her attention to the only other people in the mill.

"Hello, you two. Poor Burt, I knew there would be an accident here one day; how does the saying go, familiarity breeds contempt?"

Ant nodded.

"I didn't know you were a first-aider, Liz?" He looked at Lyn.

"No, nor me."

Liz gave a gentle smile.

"Community first responder actually, not that it matters to poor Burt. No reason why you should know. I've only just finished my training, and it's not something I tend to shout about."

"Fair play to you, Liz," responded Lyn. "This mess is certainly a baptism of fire, isn't it?"

Liz nodded and raised an eyebrow.

"You might say that, Lyn. I only do a few hours three days a week between dropping our Stephen off at school and collecting him in the afternoon, and look at what happens."

Ant mirrored the sorrow etched into his two companions' faces. "What I don't understand is how a man who uses those steps a hundred times a day, every day, makes such a silly mistake?" He could see Liz staring at him. "I know what you said about familiarity and all that, but just the same."

Ant noticed the resigned look he was getting from Lyn. "What?"

"I'll give you what. I know you, Anthony Stanton. The question is—"

Without warning, the old door to the mill seemed to

fling itself open, catching all three by surprise. A split second later the bulky frame of Detective Inspector Riley appeared, his form silhouetted by brightening sky behind him.

"I might have known it. If it isn't our very own terrible twosome, or should I say pains in the neck."

Before Ant could respond, Riley had turned his attention to Liz.

"Dead?"

"Yes, dead."

Ant could hold his temper no longer. "It's uplifting that you show such concern for Mr Bampton, Inspector. You never know; you might get an invite to the funeral.

Fool of a man.

Ant's comment stung Riley, the precise reaction he had hoped for.

"Listen, Little Lord Fauntleroy, I do this for a living, right? I don't have time for the niceties the landed gentry might enjoy. A man is dead. My job is to find out if foul play played a part in this man's demise. I'd have thought even an aristocrat could understand that."

The detective's smug tone did little to slake Ant's anger.

"Listen, you—"

Lyn cut in.

"I think what Anthony is trying to say is that he is saddened by the death of his friend. Isn't that correct?"

Ant's eyes flashed at Lyn as if a secret signal had been sent and received. His dropped his shoulders and gave her a sign he knew she would understand.

Lyn's words seem to take the wind out of Riley's sails.

"Perhaps you will allow me to get on with my job?" Riley looked at all three of them in turn. His comment passed without response.

Ant's natural inclination to bite back was suppressed by Lyn's earlier words, and the mill door being flung open for the second time in as many minutes. In stepped two paramedics, the blue lights from their ambulance providing a solemn light show for unfolding events. Ant noticed Riley had been blindsided by the sudden intrusion. He knew what was coming next as the detective fought to gain control of the situation.

"Do not touch a thing. I want this area kept sterile until Scenes of Crime have been over the area with a fine-tooth comb. So I want you all to get out."

Pompous idiot.

Stopped in their tracks, the paramedics retraced their steps until they were out of the mill. Ant led Lyn and Liz out, but not before lobbing a parting shot at Riley.

"Then you think it was an accident?"

Riley spat out his reply.

"I agree that a man lies on the floor with his head at a peculiar angle, and I doubt he is asleep. Beyond that, we shall see."

Ant felt Lyn's hand on his arm and knew what it meant. Once outside, Liz headed for the two paramedics, which Riley had unceremoniously ejected. Meanwhile, Ant and Lyn huddled against the towering mill to keep out of the wind. Ant looked across to the minibus where the Windy Wanderers had decamped to. He could just make out several faces attempting to peer through the vehicle's steamed-up windows.

Thought the driver would have put air conditioning on.

"So, what do you think? What should we do now?"

Ant pulled his coat tight under his chin and gave a shiver.

"If you want an honest answer, Lyn, we should head for

the Wherry Arms and have a drink. My mouth thinks it's been licking stamps for the last three hours—and don't look at me like that, you did ask."

Lyn shook her head as if indicating disappointment to one of her pupils.

Ant looked puzzled, "What?"

"I know what I asked, and I know what I meant."

Why can't they just say what they mean and give us a clue?

"Ah, I apologise, it was one of those questions you ask that wasn't a question at all. It was a sort of hint that I'm supposed to interpret as meaning something else, which I'm then supposed to guess the right answer to. Thank you for explaining that—not."

He got the withering look from Lyn that he expected.

"One of these days, you will understand women."

Not a chance.

Ant feigned a superior look, which gave him time to think of a suitable riposte. In the end, he decided he'd never win so carried on as if their recent conversation had never happened.

"I suppose we should tell Burt's wife what's happened?"

He could see Lyn was far from impressed.

"Anthony Stanton, you are a—"

"You two still here, then?"

So engrossed were the two friends that they hadn't noticed Detective Inspector Riley come out of the mill.

"I thought you would be looking for your next body by now. Slipping, are we?"

Ant finally had enough.

"We were talking about Burt's family if you must know." The words spat from his clenched teeth as if he resented wasting the energy in bothering to respond.

Riley bristled as he processed the intended insult.

"Don't even think about approaching the family. We will take care of that. Do I make myself clear?"

Ant spat back.

"Is that a statement, or a question, Detective Inspector?"

Lyn stepped into the fray.

"I assume you are talking about his wife, Jennifer, and their nine-year-old daughter, Sophie?"

Riley's eyes flashed; his cheeks reddened.

"I require a full statement from you two down at the station. This afternoon will do. Do you understand? And remember, stay away from the family."

The detective didn't wait for an answer. Instead, he turned on his heels and disappeared back into the mill.

"That man is insufferable."

"I have another word for him, Lyn." Ant gave Lyn a tiny nudge by way of a shared dislike of the detective. "I suppose dealing with people who lie to you day in, day out changes you. Also, I would have thought seeing the cruel results of what some people can do to others, well, I guess that must erode your feelings for people. I imagine Riley is at that point, judging by his behaviour, but wouldn't you think he would get out of the force before it does him permanent harm?"

It took Ant a second or two to understand the look Lyn was giving him.

"Yes, okay, I know. I suppose I'm the last one to talk, but at least I didn't fight the army retiring me. Out is out, isn't it?"

Lyn nudged Ant back and gave him the warmest of smiles.

"I'm guessing when the army medics said you were suffering from PTSD, you told them they were talking rubbish. Am I right?"

Ant could feel himself blushing. Only Lyn had that way of untangling how he really felt.

"Well?"

"Well, nothing. I know you better than you know yourself sometimes."

He smiled. "Only sometimes?"

Lyn smiled back. "I'm being gentle with you. Now, let's agree on what to do, and no, it's not another trick question."

Ant gave Lyn a sceptical look.

"Then I shall take your word at face value, Miss Blackthorn." He watched as Lyn shook her head and smiled. "Given the speed Riley is moving, it could be a couple of hours before he's finished here. Why don't we say our goodbyes to the Wanderers now and head off home. The police will seal this place, so it will be quite safe."

He started off towards the minibus then realised Lyn hadn't followed.

"What's up with you?"

She folded her arms as if waiting for a wayward youngster to own up to some misdemeanour or other.

"As I said, Ant, I know you better than you know yourself. Something is bothering you, so come on, out with it."

Ant thought of trying to brush Lyn's question aside but then thought better of it.

"It's just... oh, I don't know. Something is gnawing away at me about Burt's death, except I can't put my finger on it."

4
———

BROKEN BISCUITS

Saturday afternoon delivered a pleasant surprise on an otherwise sad day. The bitter easterly wind had abated to more of a chill, rather than a bone-breaking gale. Hoping to catch Detective Inspector Riley off guard, Ant and Lyn decided to attend for their interview earlier than planned.

"Afternoon, Fred."

Lyn waved a hand in greeting.

"Ah, he told me to expect you two. I don't know what on earth you've done to him, but he's in a foul mood."

The tall, rotund desk sergeant leant lazily across the high countertop of the village police station reception, an open palm cradling his ample chin.

"It doesn't take much, Fred." Lyn raised an eyebrow and tutted.

"That may be so, young lady, but it's me that gets it in the neck every few minutes with him wanting this, then that, then the thing he asked for before but forgot he'd asked." Fred blew a stream of air between a pair of downcast lips to emphasise his point.

Ant settled both forearms on his side of the countertop.

"You think he makes your life hard. He drives us two to distraction. Isn't that so, Lyn?"

"Just a bit."

Ant released his grip on the battle-worn wood surface and rummaged around in the various secret pockets of his jacket.

"I knew I had one somewhere. Here, get your teeth around that. Chocolate always seems to do the trick in times of stress."

The desk sergeant's eyes lit up as he grabbed the dark-chocolate bar, stripped it of its paper and foil covering and devoured half in one go.

"You'd better check the 'best by' date, Fred. Heaven knows how long he's had that squirrelled away."

Ant turned to confront his friend.

"Cheeky monkey, it's as fresh as the day it was made. I bought it when I last had this jacket on for that charity walk, and that was only, er..."

Ant gazed above Fred's head to a picture of Queen Elizabeth II.

"You might well look at Her Majesty for comfort, but notice the scowl she's giving you? That recent charity walk you're talking about was eight months ago."

Fred stopped chomping on his chocolate momentarily. He gave what was left of the wrapper a cursory check, before taking a second large bite of the sweet confectionery.

"Tastes all right to me," said Fred, his words garbled as he chewed on the treat.

"Men; you're all the same."

Ant took the opportunity to share a contented smile with the desk sergeant.

All is well with the world.

The cozy banter didn't last long. From the direction of

the entrance, all three were aware of a storm coming, created by a familiar voice.

"Never you mind, Betty. I'll see that horrible little man put behind bars where he belongs." Betty lagged behind Phyllis at a safe distance as was her custom when with her best friend.

"What's all this noise, then?" Fred had morphed seamlessly from cuddly cop to the stern keeper of Her Majesty's peace. "Come here, you two—and be quiet, do you hear?"

Fred's resonating baritone voice and stern look had an immediate effect. Ant and Lyn instinctively stepped back from the counter, allowing the two newcomers to approach the law.

"I want to—"

"Never mind what you want, madam. Let us start with some detail. Now, name?"

Phyllis bristled with indignation.

"You know my name, Fred Cummins, and my address. You live in the same street, remember?"

Betty tried to speak.

"My name is— "

Phyllis shot Betty a withering look.

"Do be quiet, Betty. He's playing silly beggars."

Fred pulled himself up to his full six foot four.

"Enough, ladies. It matters not that I know you. The law insists you tell me who you are and where you live if you intend to make a complaint. I assume you intend to make another complaint?"

Fred's emphasis on "another" made Phyllis bristle. Before she had a chance to fire back at Fred, a small thin man wearing a grimy orange coverall, with off-white Hi-Viz bands around the arm cuffs and midriff, dashed into the reception. Four pairs of curious eyes fell on the red-faced man. His gaze quickly settled on Phyllis.

"It's her, officer. She walloped me with her handbag— look at the size of it."

Ant hadn't noticed Phyllis' accessory before having his attention drawn to it.

Blimey, that could do some damage.

Fred's frame towered over the flustered newcomer.

"I see, sir. Are you suggesting this lady assaulted you?" The glint in the desk sergeant's eye told Ant that Fred was enjoying the prospect of arresting the elderly lady for breach of the peace.

Go for it, Fred.

"I'm suggesting this woman is crackers and needs to be kept away from the public."

Fred glared at Phyllis and toyed with the handcuffs clipped to his waistband. His action seemed to have little effect on Phyllis, who appeared to be making ready to bash the small man with her handbag for a second time.

"Don't even think about it."

Fred's wise words did the trick as the old woman settled her arm back to her side.

Fred turned his attention back to the man, whose neck had developed a blotchy appearance that stood out against his pallid complexion.

"Now, sir. What is all this about?"

"It's about— "

"Dear lady, if I have to speak to you about your behaviour again, I shall put you in a cell. Do I make myself clear?"

Phyllis turned to Betty by way of distracting Fred's attention.

"Do stop fidgeting, Betty." Betty looked suitably nonplussed.

Fred's patience had reached its limit.

"Right, you first. And you might be?"

The small man rocked back on his heels at suddenly being the centre of attention.

"I work for the Parks Department of East Norfolk District Council. This woman verbally abused me then tried to hit me with that thing." He pointed a grubby index finger at Phyllis' handbag. "All I was doing was tidying up. It was a waste of time, by the way, because of the wind. She just came at me."

Fred looked accusingly at Phyllis. Meanwhile, Ant and Lyn were enjoying the spectacle from the relative safety of a much-abused bench several feet from the counter.

"Is that the case?"

Phyllis looked at Betty, who thought she was being invited to speak, only to get as far as forming her first word before her friend dismissed the attempt.

"That horrible creature exposed himself to us, isn't that right, Betty?"

Betty perked up, having been asked a direct question.

"Well, actually, I thought you said he wolf-whistled at us."

Ant reacted in an instant as his throaty laugh bounced around the narrow reception space, aided by the painted walls and ceiling of the Victorian structure. Lyn hardly did any better as she bent forward as if admiring the red floor tiles to stifle her laughter.

Fred gave the thin man a weary look.

"What?" he replied, "Why on earth would I do that to two elderly ladies?"

Ant thought Betty looked disappointed at being written

off as too old to be admired. Phyllis simply glared at the man and tightened her grip on the handbag, ready for action.

"What you think is not important, sir. These ladies accuse you of acting in a less-than gentlemanly manner. Now, what have you to say, sir?"

Phyllis rounded on the small man.

"He's a dirty little man: that's what he should say."

Ant noticed that the elderly woman looked as if she was about to pounce.

"I'd duck if I were you."

His warning came too late as Phyllis swung her arm as if she were throwing a discus at an Olympic track and field event. The man followed Ant's advice, just managing to evade the canvas onslaught. Instead, Phyllis followed through and hit Riley, who'd shot out of his office to see what the kerfuffle was about.

"What the—"

"Sorry, sir," shouted Fred as he sped around the edge of the counter in an attempt to apprehend Phyllis, who had now lost her footing having missed her intended target.

As the little man in the orange coverall made a run for it, Phyllis lost the battle to stay upright, pushing Riley to the ground in the process. As the elderly lady realised she now lay on top of the detective, she let out a loud scream.

"Dirty little man, you're all the same. Get off me before I report you to the police."

The irony wasn't lost on Ant as he rushed forward to help Phyllis off the detective, working hard not to laugh at the sight of Riley's look of horror.

Once back on his feet, Riley let fly at Fred.

"Get these two ladies out of my police station before I nick them; report me to the police indeed." Riley turned his attention to Ant and Lyn. "And you two—my office, now."

The detective pointed to a half-glazed door with Riley's formal title stencilled on the frosted glass.

Ant looked back at Fred, causing the hapless desk sergeant to let out a little snigger. Riley caught him.

"If you don't stop doing that, you'll be on school patrol duty for the next month. Do I make myself clear?"

"THIS MUST BE the most dismal office in the universe, Lyn. Look at the state of the place. No windows, cream and brown paint. I don't think it's been decorated since Queen Victoria was a teenager."

Lyn nodded.

"But it does match Riley's temperament, don't you think?"

Ant didn't have a chance to continue what sounded like the beginning of a running joke.

"And get me a cup of tea with two chocolate digestives, and none of the broken ones."

Ant looked over his shoulder to see Riley entering the office, and in the background, Fred pulling faces at his superior as he headed for the station's tiny kitchen.

"Bad for the waistline, Detective Inspector. Do you know there are eighty-four calories in the average seventeen-gram chocolate digestive?"

He turned to see Lyn with a look of amazement on her face.

"How did you know that?" she whispered.

Meanwhile, Riley had reached his chair and curled his lip at Ant, lifted his head slightly, and sniffed the still air of his poky office.

"Now tell me what Stanton Parva's answer to Muttley

and Dick Dastardly, or should that be Laurel and Hardy, were up to at that mill?"

A second or two of silence fell across the grimy space before Ant took his time to unveil a wide smile. As he did so, he leant forward and raised a hand. Bringing his open palm down, he slapped the detective's office desk so hard that both Riley and Lyn jumped in shock.

"Detective Inspector, may I say you have such insight, such perceptiveness that I now understand why the villagers call you 'The Dog-Eared Detective.' Such a fitting name for a man we are lucky to have looking after us."

Ant watched in delight as Riley grimaced before rubbing one of his earlobes between two fingers.

"Don't you mean 'dogged,' Ant?"

"We know what I mean, don't we, Detective Inspector?"

Just as Riley was about to respond, the office door opened.

"Sorry, sir, the super ate the last of the chocolate digestives. He said you will have to make do with the Rich Tea. They're a bit soggy, but it won't matter once you dunk them, will it?"

Ant seized his moment as Fred performed a rapid retreat and closed the door as quietly as he was able.

"Good news, Detective Inspector, think of the calories you will save. I think the superintendent has your best interests at heart. Or perhaps it's just a case of her pulling rank on you?"

Ant felt a light tap on his knee and guessed Lyn was telling him to back off.

Riley scowled as he dunked his first biscuit, which broke causing the bottom half to fall back into his government-issue green cup. But not before sliding down part of the detective's tie.

"Oh dear," said Ant, feigning concern.

Lyn failed to stifle a laugh, which caused Ant to give her a concerned glance.

"No, no, Lyn. This is serious, that tie is silk. Expensive, I would suggest."

Riley's scowl deepened as he attempted to wring his tie out.

"Enough. Now tell me what you two were doing at Bampton's place this morning before I have you both locked up for perverting the course of justice."

Ant decided to push his luck.

"If you ask me, Detective Inspector, having to put up with soggy Rich Tea biscuits is the crime of a pervert."

Riley exploded, slamming his cup of tea back into its saucer and causing the contents to erupt like an Icelandic geyser.

"Get on with it."

Ant took the hint and spent the next ten minutes explaining the events leading up to Burt's fall.

"So, you didn't actually see what happened to Mr Bampton?"

Ant shook his head as did Lyn.

"No, Inspector, more's the pity. Perhaps we could have done something to prevent what happened. Who knows?"

Ant's previous levity was now replaced by a look of anguish. He leant into Lyn. She supplied the support he needed just at that moment.

"And you don't know if he had any health issues that might have caused him to fall?"

Ant shook his head.

"Well," said Lyn, "He had vertigo. I don't know if that might have had a bearing?"

"I didn't know that?" Ant's instinctive response seemed to galvanise Riley.

"So, he could have had a funny turn on a staircase so steep you need crampons on to keep a grip?"

The man has a sense of humour after all.

Ant sat back as he watched Riley retreat into a world of his own, furiously scribbling notes onto a sheet of paper contained within a manila-coloured card case file. He turned to Lyn and shot her an inquisitive look.

"I'll tell you afterwards," whispered Lyn.

Seconds felt like minutes to Ant as the detective continued to write at a furious pace, seemingly oblivious to his two visitors.

"Can we go now?"

At first, Ant thought his question would go unanswered. Then he noticed Riley's left hand lift from the desk as if waving away a troublesome child. He didn't need telling twice and gestured for Lyn to follow, leaving Riley crouched over his notes and writing as if his life depended on it.

OUTSIDE THE POLICE STATION, the crisp air offered a perfect antidote to the claustrophobic atmosphere of the detective's office. The two friends filled their lungs with clean Norfolk air and enjoyed the feeling of being free.

"What's this about Burt having vertigo? Not exactly a plus-point for working in a grain mill, is it?"

Lyn shrugged her shoulders.

"Burt mentioned it in passing months ago. I didn't think any more about it. Now I'm not so sure. Do you think he could have had a funny turn and lost his balance?"

Ant kicked a rolled-up piece of paper that the wind had

brought his way and watched it catch a gust and disappear into the distance.

"I suppose it could have happened that way, except... Oh, I don't know."

Lyn shot Ant a quizzical look. "It's not like you to give up so easily."

Her question stung. "You're right. We have to get to the bottom of this one way or another. It's clear which direction Riley is moving in. I tell you what, why don't you nip over to Burt's wife? The police will have informed her by now, and she might well do with a bit of friendly company. I'll nip over to the mill when its dark to see if I can turn anything up that might give us a clue."

Lyn nodded. "We'll need to catch up with one another to compare notes."

Ant thought for a moment. "Yes, you're right. What about a run out to Horsey to see the seals tomorrow morning after you've been to church?"

———

THE EVENING BROUGHT with it a reassuring calm as the storm passed to the west, leaving a big Norfolk sky full of stars shimmering against a deep blue canvas.

"You could've put the roof up, Ant."

Fitch pulled up the wool-covered collar of a leather flying suit around his ears and sank into the passenger seat of Ant's Morgan. "Stop moaning. We'll be at the mill in a few seconds. Anyway, I thought you liked the outdoors."

Ant took his eyes off the road long enough to grin at his old friend.

You've always been nesh.

"I may own my own motor repair place and work in all weathers, mate. Frostbite is quite another.

Fitch emphasised his point by blowing his warm breath over his distinctly blue-looking fingertips.

"I told you to grab your gloves, but would you listen? No. Do you want to borrow mine?"

Fitch shook his head. "Don't be daft."

Ant was having none of it, and as he neared a blind bend in the narrow track, he started to take his gloves off, using his knees to steer the car.

"Look out, it's going to hit us."

Fitch's shout brought Ant to his senses as he took back control and looked ahead in horror. The headlights of a car coming towards them blinded his field of view.

"Not room for both of us... only one thing to do." Ant turned the steering wheel violently to his right.

"The ditch, Ant. Watch out."

In seconds it was over. The offending vehicle roared past them and disappeared into the night, leaving the Morgan resting at an angle of almost forty-five degrees with its two offside wheels perilously close to the water. Both men sat in silence as they took in what had just happened.

"Well, thank you for such an interesting drive. What do you intend to do for an encore?"

Ant looked at his friend and laughed, more from relief than anything else. "If you've got a couple of oranges, I'm quite a juggler."

Fitch roared. Both men sat back in their seats and allowed their situation to sink in.

"I suppose we should try and get her out, Fitch."

"Suppose you're right, but I'm driving. You'll have us in the water, and I've had enough excitement for one night."

Ant gave in. Both men carefully exited the car on the

passenger side, making sure not to make any sudden movement that might send the Morgan to the bottom of the ditch.

"Careful, Ant. No saying how deep that water is. My old man used to clear ditches around here in the winter when money was tight. He reckoned some of them went three or four feet down."

Fitch's memories of his father brought their situation home. Ant gently eased himself over to where Fitch had been sitting, then out of the car. Both men now stood looking back at the Morgan.

"Did you get a look at the car, Fitch?"

His friend shook his head. "Nope, that is except for the dodgy exhaust. Did you not hear it?

Ant gave Fitch a weary look. "Er, no, I kind of had my hands full. Now come on. Get back in, and I'll push."

Fitch gently eased himself into the driver's seat and started the engine, its low rumbling tone the only sound disturbing an otherwise silent scene. "I've put it in second gear. Push when I tell you."

Ant did as he was told and pressed his weight against the back of the car, working hard to maintain his balance and not fall into the freezing water to his right.

Slowly, the Morgan reacted to Fitch's expert handling of the clutch and accelerator, aided by Ant's brute force. Two minutes later, and the car was on level ground as if nothing untoward had happened. Shortly after, Fitch brought the vehicle to a halt to one side of the mill.

As Ant scoured his beloved Morgan for damage, Fitch walked the twenty feet or so to the entrance door of the mill. He turned back to Ant.

"I don't suppose the door is supposed to be wide open?"

5

BURGLAR BILL

A nt couldn't hide his concern.

I knew something wasn't right.

Checking the lock mechanism making sure not to touch anything, Ant soon realised what they were up against.

"This is no smash-and-grab raid, or kids mucking about. Look, no damage. They must have had a key—but who? And more importantly, why?"

Realising Fitch hadn't answered, he half turned to see his friend scratching around in the narrow strip of vegetation, which surrounded the mill sides.

"Looks like Burglar Bill knew what they were doing except they were sloppy enough to drop these."

Peering into the unkempt undergrowth, Ant waited impatiently for Fitch to show his find. Separating a stand of crested buckler ferns, several odd-shaped objects glinted in the night air.

"Well, well, look what I've found."

"Don't touch them, Fitch." Ant crouched to get as close to the mysterious find as he could without knocking Fitch out of the way. "That's interesting. They're a mixture of old-fashioned lock picks and Allen keys."

"Allen keys? What's Burglar Bill doing with them? They're more useful in my garage, I'd have thought."

Ant scratched his ear, deep in thought. "Just the opposite, Fitch, these old locks need a bit of fiddling with to get them open without a key. The Allen keys provide the muscle in holding the various lever locks up, while the lock picks let you into the nooks and crannies. Now, have you a pen?"

"A pen? What on earth do you want one of those for?"

Ant held a hand up and wiggled his fingers at Fitch.

"Oh, I get it, fingerprints."

Ant offered a thumbs up as Fitch checked one pocket, then another, before finally producing a pen. Ant's reaction said it all.

"Look at the state of it. What have you been doing?"

Ant took possession of the pen between forefinger and thumb. He looked with incredulity at the gnarled plastic tip of the writing implement. A moment of silence followed as Ant continued to curl his lip at the fragment of plastic he held at a distance while inviting his friend to respond by raising his eyebrows.

"In case you've forgotten, I am a mechanic. You know, one of those people who have their head under a grimy bonnet all day, that is when we're not flat on our back with cruddy oil dripping onto our faces. Oh yes, and the type of people who get punters out of a jam because they can't drive properly."

Ant sniffed the air in dismissal of his friend's oration. "So the state of it has nothing to do with you just chewing it out of habit, you know. Like you did at school?"

He could see Fitch was rising to his friendly bait.

"Listen, do you want the pen or not? I can easily put it back in my pocket, you know."

"I suppose it will have to do."

Fitch shook his head in disbelief as Ant took a last look at the plastic tube before crouching to where his friend was still holding the vegetation apart. Acting as if trying his luck on a fairground hook-a-duck stall, Ant carefully inserted the pen through the centre of a metal ring, onto which several lock picks were attached. Retrieving the item without touching it directly, he straightened himself and held the glinting objects up to the full moon.

"I wonder if whoever owns these heard us coming, panicked, and legged it? Sound carries around these parts, and we were only a spit away."

Fitch ran his fingers through the ferns and joined Ant in examining the metal objects.

"Yes, and almost put us in a ditch."

Ant nodded.

"Exactly. I assume he didn't realise he'd dropped them, which means—"

Fitch interrupted.

"He'll be back."

"Got it in one, Fitch. Now, before we go inside for a quick shufti, can you reach into my jacket pocket? There's a paper bag, I think. Just so I can drop them inside. With a bit of luck, there may be fingerprint fragments on them."

Ant cocked his head to the right to indicate which pocket Fitch should try.

He could see the look Fitch was giving him. "What? It's only a bag for heaven's sake."

Fitch gingerly lowered his head then recoiled. "Ugh, what else have you got in there?"

Ant took a ball of white paper from Fitch and rubbed it with his right hand against his waxed jacket.

"Ah, I forgot," said Ant with a wry smile. "It's my lucky charm. I've had it since I last served in the Middle East."

Fitch frowned, his eyes fixed on the fingers of his right hand. "What the heck is it?"

Ant let out a throaty roar. "Better you don't know. Let's just say it will never bite anyone again. Now unroll this please, we need to get on."

Fitch screwed up his face as Ant handed him the paper ball.

"Are you sure that's safe to be touched by human hands?"

Ant gave his friend a wry smile. "Not at all, which means you will be quite safe."

Fitch grabbed the paper and quickly unravelled it to reveal an almost intact bag. "Hmm, it takes one to know one, and let me guess: Cornish pasty?" He tilted the open bag towards a smirking Ant.

"And jolly tasty it was too."

Fitch recovered a small piece of paper from within the bag, unfolding it to read its contents.

"This till receipt says twenty-third of September. Are you really telling me you've had that thing in your pocket for the best part of five months?"

Ant couldn't resist the temptation. "I have to leave something in there to feed my lucky charm, don't I?"

Sliding the objects with Fitch's gnarled pen into the bag, Ant took the wrapper and returned it, and its precious contents, into his jacket pocket.

"I just hope your lucky charm doesn't like metal—or you're going to be in terrible trouble with your favourite detective."

Ant smiled and patted his pocket.

"That fool, Riley, won't be getting his hands on these anytime soon. He has enough trouble tying his shoelaces."

Fitch shook his head as he followed Ant into the eerily quiet interior of the ancient mill. As he looked around the forlorn space, which was lit only by a bright moon against a cloudless night sky, Ant hoped against hope that something, anything, would jump out at him to explain why someone took the risk of breaking in.

"It looks just the same as it did when Lyn and I left, and it doesn't seem like the police disturbed anything."

Fitch was busy concentrating on not touching the entrance door with his hands as he pushed it shut.

"So why break in? It doesn't make any sense, Ant."

"I can only think of two explanations. Either they were simply chancing their arm, or they were looking for something specific."

Fitch walked the few paces necessary to join Ant.

"What's your gut feeling?"

Ant stroked his ear again, taking a few seconds to respond.

"It can't have been an off-the-cuff job. There's more than enough stuff here to get rid of on the antiques fair circuit or car-boot markets. This has got to be about retrieving something. I don't know what, but it must be important enough for whoever has been here tonight to want it back before someone else finds it."

"Then why didn't Riley turn it up, whatever 'it' is?"

"Good point, mate, but I don't think we're talking about a murder weapon. Not in the normal sense, anyway, or at least I don't believe so."

Knowing his remark served only to confuse Fitch further, Ant moved towards the wooden stairs. "You carry on looking around here. I'll do upstairs, but remember, don't touch anything. You're just looking for what isn't here, if you know what I mean?"

He turned to Fitch, who was busy shaking his head at his friend's enigmatic instructions.

"And you watch yourself up those stairs. It may be a bright night, but it's no substitute for a sunny afternoon on the beach, is it?"

Ant hesitated for a second on two accounts. First, to take in what he was doing knowing Burt had touched these same stairs for the last time but a few hours previously. Second, as he looked upwards to the first floor, he wondered at the mesmeric light and shadows being cast against the heavily timbered ceiling and odd shapes of the machinery.

Ten minutes after setting off to explore the higher floor, Ant started down the final set of steep stairs, conflicted that he hadn't found anything unusual.

What am I missing?

Adhering to the advice Burt had given him, Ant began to lower himself, front facing the narrow steps. Almost down, he let out a cry.

"Careful, Ant, watch what you're doing, or you'll end up like poor Burt."

Ant felt his friend's bulk pushing him against the steps, so stopping any chance of his slipping farther.

"Hang on, I've got you. Now, get hold of the handrails and let's get you down the last few steps."

Within a few seconds, the two men were stood in the middle of the confined floor space, looking back at the offending stairway.

"The spooky thing is, Fitch, I'm almost sure I slipped on the same step that Burt did. I was upstairs at the time, but working out where the chap above him was, I must have been within a step of where Burt's feet were."

Ant rubbed his kneecaps, both of which had caught when he began to fall.

"That hurt."

Fitch watched as his friend continued to furiously rub the offending joints.

"At least you're alive, mate."

Ant couldn't argue with Fitch's assessment. Instead, something caught his attention on the steps.

Hobbling across the ground floor, he stopped at the foot of the stairway and examined a greyish-white substance on the treads.

"This grain dust gets everywhere." Ant wiped a finger across one of the steps, which left a thin residue on his skin.

Fitch joined Ant surveying the stairway. "You can see why these places are so dangerous. That stuff's a killer, but haven't you just broken your own rule?" Fitch pointed at the finger streak on the step. What if Riley puts two and two together?"

Ant frowned, momentarily forgetting his sore kneecaps.

"Luckily, I don't think he can count, but you make a good point. We can't have him getting all excited, can we? But you can climb the damn things and clean each step on your way down."

Fitch did as he was asked then stopped to look back at Ant. "But what about all the other floors you've been on?"

Ant thought for a second. "He's too lazy to think that hard about the death. I'm sure he assumes it was down to a simple accident."

After sixty seconds of thorough dusting, Fitch cleared the final step and looked towards Ant. "You don't suppose it was an opportunist break-in after all, do you?"

Ant scanned the ground floor a final time before leading Fitch out and gently closing the heavy door with his shoulder. "You could be right, Fitch."

"DON'T you think she looks like the abominable snowman?"

Ant laughed as he watched Lyn exit the church after Sunday worship and join the vicar in talking to a small group of parishioners.

The Reverend Morton turned in the direction of the voice and smiled as the familiar figure neared.

"Ah, Anthony, nice to see you again. We missed you at the service."

Ant knew that would be the vicar's greeting and had prepared.

"We've had this discussion before, haven't we, Reverend? Perhaps, one day, but not yet."

Ant looked over to his elder brother's headstone before turning his attention back to the vicar.

"As you say, Anthony, as you say. Just know this, the church is here whenever you are ready."

Ant smiled, knowing the vicar hadn't taken offence at his directness.

"Come on, you. Let's get you in the car before you overheat in that get-up."

Lyn's smile dropped as his words hit home. "Are you telling me you've got the soft-top down on the Morgan again? I bet it's only just above freezing and you want to drive me in an open tin can?"

The small group gathered around the vicar giggled.

"It'll be fine once we get going, you won't notice it with all this sun. And actually, it's three degrees."

Ant lifted his arm to wave goodbye to the gathering as Lyn pulled the hood up of her heavy coat and tied the cord under her chin to ensure nothing would move.

"I'll three-degrees you. And I'm not talking about the pop group."

A voice chirped up from amongst the parishioners: "You're showing your age, Lyn."

Ant took his opportunity. "Always was old headed, isn't that right, Lyn."

She turned to the vicar. "You see what I have to put up with?"

Reverend Morton smiled. "At least you won't be spending your day trying to get our new camera system thingy to work. I tell you. I don't know what's worse, fending off ne'er-do-wells trying to steal lead from the roof or the so-called 'high-tech' to catch them."

Ant walked the few feet back to Lyn and gently tugged at her hand, much like a child pulling its mother away from a neighbour having waited too long for them to stop talking.

"You could always come with us to watch the seals at Horsey, Reverend."

As soon as Ant had said the words, he regretted his suggestion.

Please don't say yes.

He need not have worried.

"Alas, the computer thingy beckons. I must find out how the silly thing works before our fallen souls make a return visit and swipe the lead."

———

As the Morgan sped out of the village, the low metal-trimmed windscreen fulfilled its role of keeping the worst of the chill off the car's occupants.

"See, I told you it would be okay."

He smiled at Lyn, who was busy holding her hood as tightly into her face as possible without causing an indent on her cheeks.

"So says the man wearing a silly flying helmet. You look like Biggles without the moustache. Can you not slow down a bit, please, so that I can at least breathe?"

Ant wore his best disappointed puppy-dog look as he lifted his foot from the accelerator, allowing the Morgan to settle into a more sedate pace. "Is that better for madam?"

Lyn bit. "Don't you 'madam' me, Biggles, and if you're going to wear that silly hat, at least straighten the monstrosity. It makes your head look as though it's on the wonk."

Ant took Lyn's admonishment as a sign of grudging gratitude. He knew she would have relieved his head of its wool-lined leather flying cap and tossed it into the hedgerow, had she been really offended.

Knowing how far you can go is a good sign between friends.

Just then, Lyn reached over, grabbed his hat and threw it out of the car.

Blast.

"And I hope you have frostbitten ears by the time we get to Horsey. It'll serve you right."

He thought better of challenging her action, knowing they still had fifteen minutes until they reached their destination. Plenty of time for Lyn to engage in further mischief. Instead, he acted as if nothing had happened and tried a different tack, telling her all about the events of the previous evening at the mill.

"So you think the bloke that almost forced you into the ditch is our man?"

Ant contented himself that Lyn had come to the same initial conclusions as him. He was even more relieved she hadn't thrown anything else from the Morgan.

"Now it's your turn. How did you get on with Burt's wife? It couldn't have been easy."

Lyn rested back in the car's seat. "To be honest, she was numb. Yes, she welcomed me in, made the tea and answered my questions, but it felt more a case of lights on, no one at home."

"I get that. it must have been one heck of a shock."

Lyn nodded. "The odd thing was, she said Burt hadn't been himself for a couple of months. Apparently, he'd been wheezing and feeling tired."

Ant raised both eyebrows and tilted his head up a touch. "I bet it was all that grain dust. The place is full of it."

"You might be right, Ant, but we'll never know. Sal said she eventually made him go to the doctor, but he wouldn't tell her what Thorndike had said and says she never saw any pills. "

"Poor Sal, I wonder what she'll do now?"

Lyn brushed a leaf off Ant's arm. "Interesting you should say that because I made the same point to her. I got the impression she will sell up. Apparently, they were always getting offers, some for silly money but Burt would never sell."

As Ant brought the car to a stop on the earth-and-gravel car park, he gently tapped the steering wheel as if playing the percussion to a silent tune. "Well, I, for one, wouldn't blame her if she did sell. It must be worth a fortune, and I don't see any way Sal will want to run it, much less get some stranger in to do it for her."

Lyn pulled on a pair of woollen gloves as she got out of the Morgan and clasped her hands together. "Who knows what she'll do. For now, all I'm interested in is seeing the seals. Come on, you. I'll race you across the sand dunes."

Ant started to say he needed to get a parking ticket from the machine first, except Lyn didn't hear him; she'd already taken off. By the time he'd stuck the receipt to the windscreen and secured the Morgan's soft-top in position, Lyn was waving back at him from the top of the dune.

As Ant made towards Lyn, he realised he'd underestimated how difficult the sand was to run on. Now he was paying for attempting to do it at pace.

"You really are out of shape, Ant. Just listen to your breathing."

He bent forward and placed a hand on each knee as if stopping himself from falling over. "Listen, you. I've... I—"

Lyn laughed as Ant tried in vain to get his words out. "I'd give it a minute if I were you. I don't want you keeling over on me. That car of yours has a mind of its own, so I don't really want to have to drive us back to the village."

Ant tried, and failed, to catch his breath quickly enough to make the retort he had in mind in any way effectively. Instead, he practised a breathing technique the army had taught him to recover from overexertion.

Not eighteen anymore.

"Better?"

"Don't know what you mean, Lyn. Fit as a fiddle, me."

He raced ahead, stealing a few seconds on his amused friend.

"Taking advantage, that's what I call it," shouted Lyn as she raced to catch him up and be first to the viewing platform twenty-five yards ahead.

Ant didn't take kindly to being overtaken, let alone beaten to their destination. Extending an arm in an attempt to bar Lyn's way, and failing, he tried a final spurt of speed, to no avail.

"What took you so long, Mr Cheater?"

Lyn's face said it all. Ant avoided eye contact.

You always won at school. Some things never change.

While Ant took his time to get his breath back, Lyn looked out onto the white horses of the North Sea, then shortened her gaze into the mass of seals with pups close to their mothers along the sandy coastal strip for as far as the eye could see. Steam rose from the heavily insulated bodies of the creatures, and an occasional roar came from bulls fighting for dominance. Meanwhile, a menagerie of squeals came from several hundred pups as they struggled to stay out of trouble from fighting males and territorial females.

Ant's need to gulp air suffered from a considerable hurdle.

"What in the name of sanity is that smell?"

Lyn beamed with amused delight.

"What smell? I can't smell a thing."

Ant finally pulled himself upright by letting go of his kneecaps and pointed at the bobbing mass of blubber to his front and sides.

"Are you mad? You're expecting me to believe you can't whiff that lot?" Ant pointed an accusing forefinger at the oblivious wildlife.

Lyn gave an exaggerated sniff of the air. "Nope, all I can detect is the perfume of life." Her smile grew broader as she took in the scene.

Ant shook his head in disbelief, his forefinger now wagging like a headmaster demanding his orders be carried out by his sniggering charges. "Perfume of life? You're bonkers, you are. They stink. It's lost on me how something that pongs so much can be attracted to another Whiffy

Wally. Oh, wait a minute, I know how they do it. They're nose-blind."

"Nose-blind?"

"Yep, nose-blind. You know, like when you go into the changing room at your school after fifty kids have been running around the field for an hour in summer, ugh!" Ant gave Lyn a questioning look.

"What are you talking about?"

"There, that proves my point."

Yes, get in.

Before Lyn could answer, Ant's mobile rang. Putting the oblong piece of plastic close to his ear to screen out the onshore wind, he nodded, then looked at Lyn.

"Are you sure? I see, yes. Okay, one of us will get around as soon as we can."

By the time Ant placed the phone back in his pocket, Lyn was near to bursting with anticipation.

"That was Fitch. He's just fitted a new exhaust to a car that he reckons sounded like the one that almost put us in a ditch last night."

6

FLYING CAPS

"I should be so lucky. Easy afternoon, indeed. I've got hours of marking ahead of me and an agenda to put together for my staff meeting tomorrow afternoon."

Ant grinned as he brought the Morgan to a stop outside Schoolhouse Cottage. "Marking? You mean ticking a few sums your six-year-olds did for you on Friday. Call that work?"

He interpreted her pointing to where his flying helmet had sat as a hint that his travelling companion meant business.

"It won't just be your silly hat next time, Anthony Stanton. You can mark the children's work if you think it's so easy. I'll have a leisurely shower, knock my agenda up, and spend the rest of the afternoon reading a cozy mystery. What do you think?"

Not on your nelly.

Ant switched off the ignition. "Er, I would, only—"

"Only you are a coward. Was that what you were going to say, Lord Stanton?"

Now Ant knew he was in real trouble with Lyn.

Think, stupid, think.

His moment of hesitation passed. "Not at all. I think I can best use my time by nipping over to Fitch's garage to see what he knows about our mysterious exhaust man."

He waited a few seconds before daring to gauge Lyn's reaction. Placing a hand on top of his head to keep his cap safe from kidnap, Ant looked sideways before the pain in his eye sockets made him move his head so that she was in full view. To his horror, Lyn was about to write on a scrap of paper resting on the leather-covered dashboard.

"Lyn, what are you—"

She lifted her pen from the paper, and instead, scribbled the note on her lap using a small road atlas from the door pocket to rest on. "Ah, so I've got your attention, then. Don't worry, I know putting a mark on any part of your silly car constitutes a capital crime."

Immediate danger over, he ran his hand over where Lyn had placed the paper, checking for indents or ink stains. "That wasn't funny."

"No, neither was taking the mick out of my pupils' work."

Ant shook his head.

Wish she would stop changing the rules.

"I was only joking, Lyn."

"And I was only joking pretending to write on your daft leather."

Fair play.

Ant broke into a gentle smile and gestured to see what she had written. He lifted the square of paper and digested its contents. It didn't take him long: Men Are Stupid.

"Right, young Anthony. I'm off for my shower and get on with my marking. I'll call over to the Hall this evening to bring your parents their cake and catch up with you. Off you go to Fitch's, then."

I think that's what you call being dismissed.

IN THE TWENTY-FIVE seconds it took for Ant to drive from Lyn's place to Fitch's Automotive Services, he accepted Lyn's wrath as a lesson learnt. Clearing the final sharp bend before entering the street, he caught sight of Fitch with his upper torso half in and half out of the engine compartment of an ancient Land Rover.

Pulling onto the garage forecourt, Ant had to shout to make himself heard over the spluttering engine of the Land Rover. "Sounds like a sack of old iron being shaken by a bear with bronchitis."

It took a few seconds for Fitch to extract himself from the inner workings of the old vehicle. Using an oily rag to wipe his hands, Fitch screwed the scrap of cloth into a tight ball and shoved it into a pocket in his equally oily coveralls.

"You know whose it is, don't you?" Fitch looked back at the dented body shell and shook his head.

Ant leant out of his Morgan and took in the pitiful state of the Land Rover. "Let me see. It wouldn't be old Mycroft's, would it?"

Fitch nodded. "Give that man a fish."

"It would take more than a fish to get me behind the wheel of that thing." Ant dismissed the crumpled vehicle with a wave of his hand.

"I wouldn't mind, but the old miser has got more money than me, Lyn, and you, put together. He hesitated. "Well, me and Lyn anyway."

Ant offered a wry smile as he rested his right arm on the

door frame of the Morgan and looked up at Fitch, who had moved to within a few feet of his friend. "The storage business must pay well, that's all I can say. He must have, what, a couple of hundred caravans and motorhomes in store there? To say nothing of all those containers. That's got to be a better option than keeping a seventeenth century Tudor wreck going, that's for sure."

Fitch made as if to play an imaginary violin. "Don't expect me to have any sympathy for you, mate. I'd hardly call Stanton Manor a wreck. Okay, so you need a few buckets when it rains, and the electricity bill must be a stinger, but it's hardly falling down, is it?"

Ant raised his eyebrows and huffed. "Feels like it sometimes, Fitch. Anyway, talking about wrecks, fill me in on Exhaust Man."

Just then a slim teenager with her jet-black hair tied back into a bun strolled out of the garage workshop. "I've done the—" She froze as she caught sight of Ant.

"Good to see you again, Rachel. How's this old rogue treating you?"

The girl looked at Fitch, then Ant, then back at Fitch.

"Come on over, then. He's not going to bite. Not least he hasn't got the teeth for it anymore."

Ant smiled at Rachel, which encouraged the teenager to approach the two men.

Fitch grinned at Rachel. "She's coming along nicely. And she makes a better cup of tea than you, mate."

Rachel blushed as her attention turned back to Ant. "I like it here... and I go to college in Norwich one day a week to get my City and Guilds qualifications. Level two at the moment, but I hope to go for my level three next September."

Ant's smile broadened as the words tumbled from the apprentice. "I'm so glad to hear that, Rachel. You never know, Fitch might be making the tea for you one day instead of the other way around." He pointed a finger at his friend to reinforce his point.

Rachel's blush intensified. "Oh, I dunno about that. But I do intend to be a good mechanic. I know that."

That's the spirit.

"Anyhow, enough of this talking," said Fitch, pointing back to the workshop. "Why don't you get on with changing the oil and filters on the blue Ford Focus. He'll be in for it later today, so we need to get a move on."

Rachel nodded, turned, and headed back to the workshop. Then she stopped, turning her head towards Ant. "And I want to do you proud, Mr Anthony. I won't forget what you did for me." She turned back towards the workshop and disappeared without waiting for Ant to respond.

Fitch tilted his head at Ant. "It's going well. I know I said you were mad, and I have to admit I wasn't best pleased when you dropped her on me. But you know what, it's good to have an apprentice around here again."

Ant gave his friend the broadest of grins. "Well, you old softie, who'd have thought this oily metal-twiddler had a heart. I should watch out, Fitch. If word gets out, you'll never live it down. Anyway, I had an ulterior motive. It was one way of stopping her and her partner in crime from stripping any more lead from the estate."

Fitch returned his friend's smile. "Now, who's a softie, and speaking of Rachel's mate, how's he getting on?"

"The vet said he'd never had such a keen trainee. Just goes to show you, Fitch. Give these youngsters a chance, and they'll bite your arm off."

Fitch dug the oily rag from his pocket, bunched it up, and tossed it at Ant. "So you really are an old softie."

Ant caught the rag mid-flight and tossed it straight back at his friend. "Not so much of the 'old.' Now, you were telling me about that noisy exhaust you changed. Got an address for me, then?"

Fitch's smile melted away as they got back down to business. "The thing is, Ant, it was a cash-in-hand job. You know, no receipt, like."

"Hmm. That will make things harder, but you must have got a look at the number plate, and what did the fella look like? How did the man behave?"

The barrage of questions took Fitch by surprise. "Whoa, slow down, mate, let me think. You gotta remember I didn't think anything of it at first. It was only when he'd gone that I started thinking, and that's when I rang you."

Oops, gone in too heavy again.

A passing villager calling out to the two men and wishing them a pleasant day gave Fitch the few seconds he needed to gather his thoughts.

"Well, I reckon he was about twenty-five. Sharp dresser and going by the amount of time he spent looking in his wing mirror, more than a bit vain, I'd say."

"Did he talk to you much? You know what most lads of that age think about their car. He must have said something other than fix my exhaust, mate?"

Fitch shook his head. "That was the strange thing. You know how chatty almost everyone in the village is even if it's only to find out or pass on the latest gossip, well, this chap hardly said a word. In fact, when I asked him how long his exhaust had been blowing and the like, he just shrugged his shoulders. It was as if he didn't want to let on who he was, but he must be fairly local to have tipped up here."

Ant rubbed his chin with two fingers. "I agree, though if you'd broke into the mill, would you stay local? Then again, hiding in plain sight works time and time again. Most people expect scallywags to do a runner after doing a job, but what if our chappy is cleverer than that? Either way, he's managed to turn up here, get his car fixed, and vanish into thin air in less than an hour." Ant turned the ignition key to bring the Morgan to life. "Don't suppose you can remember the make of the car?"

Fitch smiled. "Of course I can. I'm a mechanic, aren't I?" He waited for Ant to acknowledge the fact. He didn't. "Hmm, anyway, it was a 2010 white Alfa Romeo Giulietta, a good little hot hatchback in its time, let me tell you. Not much space inside, mind, but they go like the wind. And before you ask again, yes, I did get a snippet of the number plate. It started with an L and had fifty-nine in the number sequence. That means it was first registered in the early part of 2010 in London. Will that do?"

Respect, my friend.

Ant couldn't help but show his surprise. "As you say, you are a mechanic after all. Well done, Fitch. At least that gives me something to go on. I'll see whether one of my contacts can trace it for us. You never know, we may get lucky."

Engaging first gear and easing the handbrake off, Ant gave the accelerator the gentlest of touches to enable the Morgan to ease forward. Fitch began to shout as the engine gave off its signature low rumble.

"So you think the boy-racer could be our man?"

Ant made a final check of his mirrors before pressing harder on the accelerator. "Let's not get ahead of ourselves, but that lad is hiding something, or maybe he's just an anti-social millennial. Time and a little bit of digging will tell, Fitch."

"ONE OF THESE days perhaps you will permit me to win." Ant looked forlornly at the oak scoreboard on the wall of Stanton Hall's billiard room. He didn't like the look of it. "Who taught you to snooker the opposition like that?"

Lyn blew the excess chalk from the tip of her cue as she bent forward to play the next shot. "Actually, it was your father. Gerald was very patient with me while you were away playing soldiers, and I think he liked the company. Anyway, I don't always win." She smiled as her cue made contact with the white cue ball with a satisfying "click," which sent it on its way to sink the blue in the far corner of the vast green baize-covered snooker table.

I should have guessed.

"You are correct to say I have beaten you, but that was years ago, and I've rather forgotten how it feels. I suppose all that mentoring Dad gave you was because of all the cakes you make for my parents. Oh, by the way, they said to thank you for your latest creation. Not that I got a sniff of it."

Lyn stood ramrod straight, having fluffed her latest shot. Placing her cue gently on the green felt, she put a hand on each hip. "Giving compliments to a lady when she's trying to concentrate constitutes cheating, Anthony Stanton."

He grinned as he watched Lyn's cue ball sink into a middle pocket. "Oh dear. I had no idea you were about to take a shot. I was looking at the scoreboard. Never mind, fancy a drink?"

Lyn wagged a playful finger as she followed Ant to two low burgundy leather chairs placed opposite one another at the far end of the vast room. A small circular oak table rested between them. A silver tray with two deep-cut crystal whisky glasses and matching decanter completed the arrangement.

"How are your parents? I meant to call in all week, but well, you know, stuff gets in the way."

Ant poured two whiskies and handed one to Lyn as she sank back into her chair. "They were sorry to have missed you when you arrived. Neither like being stuck in bed, but at least the cake cheered them up a bit. You know Mum and Dad, they like to be out and about, and you'll never hear them complaining. But I notice things. We don't talk much about their health, but you know it's a worry."

Lyn gave a slight nod as she took the first sip of her single malt. "I know. It must be hard, and I know you worry a lot about them. The thing is, Ant, you still have them. That's a blessing in itself, yes?"

You know how to hit the spot.

"Yes, I know that, but all the same we think our parents will go on forever, don't we?" Ant gazed into his glass, which sparkled in the soft light of the log fire, lost in his own thoughts. "But there will come a day when that phone call comes. You must dread it too?"

Lyn leant forward and placed her glass back on the small table which separated them. "Yes, but not for the same reasons you do with your parents, at least not the only reason." She looked at Ant without blinking, waiting for his response.

Bullseye again, Lyn.

"The estate."

Lyn held out her hand. Ant reciprocated, their fingers lightly touching each other. "It's a big responsibility, I know, but you are up to it. Your dad would have made different arrangements if he didn't think so. You know that, don't you?"

Ant didn't answer. A look between the pair was enough. He let go of Lyn's fingers and settled back into his chair.

Time to change the subject.

"I forgot to mention. I met with the architects the other day. You know, about setting up a training school for teenagers in the old stables."

Lyn smiled. "Ah, that's another thing I've been meaning to catch up on. How did it go?"

Ant recovered his glass from the table and took a sip. "Surprisingly well. In fact, he thinks we will qualify for a grant to cover about half the cost. The idea is to work with local colleges to training young lads and lassies in everything from land management to building conservation. The only problem we might have is with the planning authorities."

Lyn's eyes sparkled as her passion for education shone through. "I know this place is grade-two listed, but you would have thought to put an unused stable block, no matter how grand, to good use should make getting planning permission easy."

Ant gave a throaty laugh. "I agree, but planning officers involved in listed planning consent are a different breed. To make matters worse, you get a different view depending on which one of them you talk to. But as my architect keeps reminding me, there's nothing to be gained by arguing with them, just the opposite, in fact."

"Talking about listed buildings, have you had any further thoughts about the mill and what happened to Burt?"

Ant swirled the remainder of this whisky around the crystal tumbler before finishing it off in one go. "Well, I spoke to Fitch about the bloke with the dodgy exhaust. Not much to go on, but he gave me enough to carry on digging.

As for whether Burt's death was an accident or not, I can still make a case for either scenario, and it's not a position I like being in. Either way, we'll soon have to decide, because Riley will shut this case down if he gets half a chance. If we are to push the murder angle, we need to be sure of our facts before squaring up to our beloved detective inspector."

Offering Lyn a top-up of her drink, Ant walked the few feet from his chair to the Adams-style fireplace and warmed his hands in the glowing embers. "What we do know is that the mill is a dangerous place to be around. Also, Burt hadn't been well, and I can well imagine it gave him a dicky chest. But—"

Lyn cut across her friend. "Hypersensitivity pneumonitis."

"What?"

"Hypersensitivity pneumonitis. It's also known as miller's lung. A wheat weevil called Sitophilus granarius causes the grain dust to become contaminated. Nasty stuff by the sound of it—but we've no proof it's present at the mill."

Ant couldn't take his eyes off Lyn as she explained the effects of the condition on the human lung. "Wow, the name is enough to take your breath away, never mind that pesky weevil. But you're right. We have no evidence it affected Burt, and I doubt very much that the police will be considering any such thing. However, perhaps I can get a sample to one or two friends and pull a few strings. At least that way, we can count it in or out as a cause of Burt's ill health, which might help his wife come to terms with what's happened. So what else have we got?"

The two friends spent the next ten minutes sifting through what they already knew, or thought they knew, about events leading up to Burt's death."

"So we're agreed, Lyn. You will focus on Ron Busby, and I'll see if I can find our reclusive exhaust man, and have a chat with Albert Sidcup. You never know; we might get lucky."

Lyn nodded. "For Burt's sake, I do hope so."

7

INSURANCE

Pleased to find a parking space in the large market square, Ant brought his Morgan to a stop within a few yards of an imposing buttercross. He spent a few seconds admiring its lead-covered dome capping supported on eight elegant stone columns.

Lovely place, but thank heavens it's not Saturday.

Swaffham had a well-earned reputation for being difficult to park in on market day, which he was pleased to have avoided. As he made his way on foot to Albert Sidcup's place of work, he gazed around the large square with its range of Georgian buildings and thought about the town's few, but important, claims to fame.

To think Howard Carter left here and found Tutankhamen's burial site. Almost as important as that TV series, Kingdom, *filmed here with Stephen Fry.*

As he passed the shop used as Fry's fictional solicitor's office, Ant squinted in the cold morning sun as he scoured the landscape for "Sidcup's Independent Insurance Brokerage."

Business must be bad: the shop's falling to bits.

Standing in front of the old building adorned with flaking cream paint and rotted window frames, he approached the door, unsure if it would withstand the shock of being opened. As he entered, an old-fashioned bell rang out, reminding Ant of a Dickens novel.

Scrooge, or The Old Curiosity Shop.

The interior of the establishment looked in no better shape than its exterior. Bits of old paint hung lazily from the ceiling and walls; posters extolling the virtue of life insurance, and two shabby wood chairs completed the look. In one corner of the small office sat the tall figure of Albert Sidcup behind a leather-covered desk that Ant thought far too big for the space available. Peering over his rimless glasses, Albert twiddled with his pen.

"Ah, Mr, or should I say, Lord Stanton. How nice to see you."

Ant smiled as he sauntered over to a carver chair Sidcup was pointing to on the opposite side of his vast desk. "Ant, or Anthony, if you must, will do fine. May I call you Albert?"

Sidcup offered a nervous smile. "I take it you are here to discuss those awful events of Saturday? Poor Mr Bampton, such a tragedy." Albert picked up his pen again and started to twirl it between his stubby fingers.

"How's business? I do hope the good folks of Swaffham are taking the advice of your insurance posters and getting themselves covered by you."

Let's see how easily you're rattled.

The question resulted in Albert's involuntary intake of breath, forcing his lips to part just enough to bare his teeth. He quickly regained control. "Well, it's certainly the case that it's never too late to take out the right insurance policy. None of us knows what's around the corner, do we?"

The good people of Swaffham don't seem to agree with you.

Ant nodded. Lyn taught him the value of demonstrating active listening, even if his usual sort of interaction called more for a deadly weapon aimed at the enemy than polite conversation. "That's good to hear, Albert. Then business is good?"

Sidcup tensed. His body language told Ant all he needed to know.

A bit short of cash, then.

Sidcup rose from his faux leather swivel chair and gestured towards a coffee percolator bubbling away on a rickety table in the adjacent corner of the room.

"Wonderful, yes please, no milk and one sugar, if you will."

In the few seconds Sidcup's back was turned as he wiped two mugs clean and filled them with steaming coffee, Ant took the opportunity to scan the papers on the desk. Reading upside down was another skill Lyn had taught him.

They don't print final demands in red anymore, but you can still spot them a mile away.

"There we are. You said one sugar, yes?"

Ant nodded as he took the hot drink from Sidcup and watched the man slump back into his chair. "Thank you, that's so kind." He then purposely stopped talking to see how Sidcup might react. Ant's hunch was correct: the longer the silence continued, the more agitated Sidcup became.

"So, we were talking about poor Mr Bampton."

Sidcup's hesitant sentence opened the way for Ant to press harder.

"As you say, Albert, a tragedy, not least for his poor wife and child. One wonders how they will manage now."

Come on, Albert, my hook is waiting.

He watched as a puzzled expression spread across the man's face.

"Manage? How do you mean, Lord, er, Anthony? She has the mill. Must be worth a fortune, and I'm sure he must have had life assurance in place."

Thank you, Albert

"I doubt Burt's wife is thinking about such things just at the moment, do you? I simply meant what a difficult time she must be having processing her husband's death—if, indeed, it's possible to process such a thing."

Ant's professional background came to the fore. It wasn't that he wanted the man to feel uncomfortable for the sake of it. He was following his instinct in getting the truth out of an adversary.

"No, no. Yes, of course. I didn't mean for one moment that, er. Oh dear, what must you think of me."

Excellent, that'll do for now.

"Now, now, Albert. I don't think anything. I'm just trying to make sense of this tragedy and thought you may be able to give me a little background on the Windy Wanderers' visit to the mill?"

Sidcup took a few seconds to compose himself. He grabbed at his coffee mug and tipped some of its contents onto the table as he nervously began to lift the drink to his lips.

"Not to worry, Albert. I have some tissues. My mother always insists I carry them, saying you never know when you'll need them. As usual, she's right." He dabbed the trail of liquid from the table as far as Sidcup's tie. "Here, let me take the mug and clean it for you."

Sidcup's hand was left in mid-air as Ant took control of the brightly coloured container. He wiped the dregs of coffee from its base and placed it back onto the table in front of the still bemused insurance broker. "There now, isn't that better? Now, you were telling me about the visit."

You're mine now.

A torrent of words streamed from the man.

"And they want to visit every grain and watermill in Norfolk. The trouble is no one wants to organise them, so it's left to muggins here to do all the running about and..." The man finally took a breath before continuing at a slightly slower pace. "And it's not as if I haven't enough to do, what with the business and everything. It's all right for most of the others: they're retired on a nice income, so they can just swan about the place like they're on permanent holiday. I, on the other hand, need to—" Sidcup's voice stalled.

Earn enough to pay off debts judging by the final demands on the desk.

The insurance broker took in a deep breath before continuing with his soul-bearing outburst. "Every year at our annual general meeting, I ask for someone else to take on the role of events secretary. Do any of them volunteer? Never. They just say I do such a good job, and it would be wrong to take it off me. What am I to do?"

You sound an angry man to me.

"I see your point, Albert. Tell you what, why don't I do us a refill? I think we both need another coffee, don't you?" He didn't wait for a reply; instead, he retrieved Sidcup's mug, and along with his own, walked the few feet to the still bubbling percolator. "Here, drink this while you take a break. I can see what hard work the group means for you. And you're right, people are only too willing to let others carry the load. I'd feel just like you if I was in your shoes. You know, not wanting to let anyone down and all that. Likely that means neglecting important business and costing you money most of us can't afford to lose."

Sidcup relaxed back into his chair and took several sips of his coffee, blowing on his mug each time to cool the dark liquid. "You're right, Anthony. I can see we have a lot in common."

Oh no we don't.

"Exactly, Albert. Take how dangerous that mill is, not least as windy as it was when Ron fell into Burt on the decking. Who knows if he had any life insurance in place?"

Sidcup stiffened and gripped his coffee mug tight against his chest, its steaming contents billowing onto his chin and beyond.

"Why would I wish Mr Bampton to fall? It's not as if I have any interest in the mill."

Strange thing to say.

Ant took a sip of his coffee, deliberately taking his time all the while staring unblinkingly at Sidcup. "The thing is, Albert, the police may take a different view. You know what they're like, always looking for someone to charge to improve their clear-up rate. I've had a few run-ins with that Riley fellow, I can tell you. Nasty piece of work. Have they spoken to you yet?"

The question made Sidcup choke on the mouthful of coffee he'd just taken.

"Yes, I mean no, well, er, yes, that detective chap did speak to me. He spoke to all of us. He just asked about where I was when Mr Bampton had his accident, that's all. And as for the rest of the group, don't be fooled. They can be a nasty lot, little cliques all over the place. And do they like gossiping? I don't know why I bother staying in the thing. No one likes me."

Seems more interested in the group than the police.

"You're not suggesting some of the group thinks you kept

arguing with Burt on purpose, are you?" Ant's upward inflexion on the end of his sentence had the desired effect.

"Too right, they do. Especially that Ron Busby, a nasty piece of work, that one."

Sidcup's fingers turned white as he grabbed his coffee mug so tightly that Ant thought the handle might come off.

"How awful, but why do you think Mr Busby feels like that towards you?"

Sidcup took his time putting the mug back on its coaster and leant forward so that his elbows now rested on the plum-coloured leather desktop.

"Because he's jealous, that's why." Sidcup settled back into his chair with what Ant swore was a look of self-satisfaction.

Wonder where this will take us?

"Albert, when men speak the way you have, experience tells me there's usually a woman involved?" Ant kept his gaze firmly on Sidcup, looking for any clues the man might inadvertently offer up.

"As you say, Anthony."

Well, well, a love tryst within the Windy Wanderers.

Ant took his time in replying. He wanted Sidcup to savour the moment before bursting his bubble. "Oh dear, I had no intention of prying into personal matters."

That brought a smile to your face, matey. Let's knock you off balance.

"The thing is, Albert, the fact is you kept firing questions at Burt about how much the mill was worth and all that. Can you see how that looks? You know, insisting he tells you if he'd ever thought of selling the place. You can see how it might look to the police, and as you say, some of the Windy Wanderers are jealous of you. Is there anything you can help me with before the police put two and two together and make five?"

Sidcup's grin of contentment vanished in a second.

"Lord Stanton. I always found Mr Busby to be a gentleman, whether dealing with him on Wanderers' business or in a professional capacity. I had—"

The desk telephone rang.

"I'm sorry. I must take this call." Sidcup gestured towards the door. Ant took the hint.

"Sorry I'm late, Mr Busby. I had a little problem to sort out between a couple of my year twos; you know how children can be." Lyn smiled as Ron Busby showed her into to his neat bungalow five miles south of Aylsham. "So kind of you to see me at such short notice, but I wanted to feel the waters, as they say, about how the Windy Wanderers might wish to mark Burt's passing."

Lyn watched as Busby glanced at a long, narrow hall mirror as he passed and rearranged his comb-over.

"Well, I'll be blowed, if ever there was a case of serendipity, it's now. I have been talking to some of the group, and they suggested we do exactly as you suggest. Now, please, come into the lounge and take a seat. Would you like a drink?"

She followed Busby into the small lounge made to look all the smaller by a colossal pine Welsh dresser against one wall and a dated, coloured brick fireplace opposite. "That's so kind of you, but no. I don't want to take too much of your time."

Busby sat on a brown dralon-covered armchair and gestured for his visitor to sit opposite him. "Not at all, I'm happy to meet with you... er, perhaps happy is the wrong word to use in the circumstances. I'm sure you know what I mean, Miss Blackthorn."

"Oh, Lyn, please, I get quite enough of my formal name from a hundred and forty little ones each day." She smiled at Busby then glanced around the room. "You have a lovely home, Ron... may I call you Ron?"

The man smiled back, which she took to mean permission had been given.

"It was my mother's place. I came back here in the seventies after my father died and somehow found myself staying. She missed him terribly and wouldn't allow anything to be changed, so it's more than a little dated."

"I'm sorry, Ron. I didn't mean to—"

"Please, Lyn, it's fine. Mother died last year, so it's about time I did the place up, but when living alone, it's hard to get up the motivation. Perhaps it needs a woman about the place."

She smiled as Busby waved a hand to gesture at the general state of the room. "So have you any ideas on how the group might want to mark Burt's passing?"

Lyn's question brought Busby's focus back to his visitor. "I've received various ideas from the group. These range from a simple flower tribute at the funeral to some kind of a plaque on the mill noting Mr Bampton's contribution to the conservation of the broads. That's if his widow agrees, of course."

What a lovely thought.

"I think Mrs Bampton would be delighted. Would you like me to broach the subject with her?" Lyn immediately realised she'd said the right thing, judging by the relief spreading over Busby's face.

"Would you? That's wonderful. None of us has met her, so I'm sure the lady will react more favourably to you."

Right, let's get to it.

"Of course. Delighted to help. Ron, there was one other thing I wanted to discuss with you. I know that the police spoke to you on that terrible day. The thing is, I hear rumours that they think Burt may have been murdered and have found a bruise on his left collarbone. I just wanted to warn you that they may wish to speak to you again."

A little white lie can't hurt, can it?

Busby shot from his chair and made for the wide picture window. As far as Lyn could determine, he wasn't looking at anything in particular. "Ron, are you okay?"

After what seemed like an age, Busby turned to face Lyn. Gone was the easy smile, which was now replaced with ill-disguised fury. She noticed a tiny tremor in his bottom lip, made all the more noticeable by him incessantly licking his lips. It reminded her of a dog a friend once had, which would, on occasion, continuously pace the room, take a sip of water after each circuit, lick its lips then yawn. She learnt to her cost that the signs meant the animal was feeling threatened and ready for a fight.

"What has that got to do with me, Miss Blackthorn?"

Lyn noted the return to formality. "I don't know, except they know you were directly above Burt on the steps, and that you were on the top decking when he almost fell over the edge. I'm just keen that you know what might be coming so that you can defend yourself."

Lyn wasn't prepared for Busby's reaction.

"So that's why you've come here today. Nothing to do with Mr Bampton's death, or at least celebrating his life. You think I had something to do with the man's demise. How dare you! What right have you to accuse me?"

Thinking he was about to go for her, Lyn jumped up from her chair and made for the front door. "Ron, I said no such thing. I meant no such thing. I—"

"I know what you meant. You are all the same. You think you know better than us. Well, let me tell you, you do not. I had nothing to do with that man's death. I can assure you that if I had wanted him dead, there are many better ways to have done it. Now come back here. You will listen to what I have to say, or..."

Lyn didn't wait for Busby to finish his sentence. Instead, she reached for the Yale lock, twisted the knob, flung the front door wide open, and made for her MINI Clubman. Glancing back, Lyn saw Busby at the open doorway, his face still contorted with rage. She was thankful he made no effort to bar her escape.

"YES, I'm on my way home now, Ant. The man went crazy. Can you come over? Good, I'll see you in an hour." Lyn pressed the end call button on the steering column and shifted down a gear as she put as much distance between her car and Busby in the shortest possible time.

"I'VE TOLD YOU, Ant. I thought I had things under control, then he just went crazy. I've never seen anyone turn so quickly. My dad has a temper, but nothing like that."

Ant pushed a glass of white wine across Lyn's kitchen table and gestured for her to drink. "Go on, you deserve it. Must have been terrifying for you?"

Lyn finished her drink off in one go and held the glass

out for Ant to refill. "You've no idea. I never want to be in that position again. You'd think I'd be used to it with irate parents tipping up at my office at least twice a week, but at least at school, I'm the one in charge, so I can handle it. Busby's place was another thing entirely."

Ant emptied the last of the bottle as he refilled Lyn's glass and topped his own up. The pair spent the next ten minutes filling each other in on their separate meetings.

"So, that means we have two men on our hands with a temper. The question is, Lyn, was either of them angry enough with something to have killed Burt?"

"Or might they be in it together?"

8

FIRST AID

"Hands up who would know what to do if one of your friends suddenly had a nosebleed?"

In an instant, a dozen hands shot up as Lyn addressed her pupils at morning assembly. The school hall was flooded with light from a bright sun shining through the large windows. The sills were just above the average height of a ten-year-old to discourage inattention caused by little minds wandering as they peeked out to see what the world was up to.

"Yes, Terrence Woodman, you seem quite keen to tell us, so on your feet, and explain to everyone what you would do."

The seven-year-old unfolded himself from that cross-legged sitting position only possible when you are at primary school. "Please, miss, my mum says you should bend their heads back and put a bunch of keys down their shirt."

Terrence's remedy met with derision amongst the majority of his peers. A surge of laughter rang out, causing the teachers sat around the perimeter of the room to stretch out their arms and gesture for quiet as if it were a choreo-graphed routine. In the end, Lyn took charge, and with the raising of one finger to her lips restored calm within seconds.

"That's not very nice, is it, children. Terrence has been brave enough to put his hand up, unlike you, Keith Fleming. It's all well and good to poke fun at someone when you aren't brave enough to do it yourself." Keith Fleming, cock of the school, looked suitably chastened. He was not someone who enjoyed the spotlight unless he was picking a fight with someone he could beat.

Terrence decided he'd had enough. "Don't care, that's what my mum says, and she knows everything in the world." With that, he folded his arms across his chest and scanned his peers in defiance.

Lyn noted that several of the children, mostly girls, appeared impressed with Terrence's bold stance as their gaze shifted from Terrence to Keith Fleming and back to Terrence. Keith seemed to be forlorn, a state Lyn knew she would have to watch in case he lashed out at Terrence or anyone else who attempted to slight him as the school day progressed.

"All right, all right, children. That will do. Now, Terrence's remedy may be a good approach, but what if you don't have any keys?" A hundred and forty young faces morphed into deep thought as they pondered such a situa-tion. "Well, we are lucky enough to have with us this morning an expert who has come to talk to us about first aid. That's what we call it when we have a little cut that needs treating, or we fall off our bike and scuff our knee."

The children's faces lit up with excitement as the double doors to the school hall opened, and in walked a figure dressed in a luminescent yellow jacket and trousers, head completely covered by a motorbike helmet with black visor, and carrying a colossal backpack.

"Now, I want you all to give a big round of applause for Mrs Wilson. Our visitor today is called a community first responder. And as you can tell, children, Mrs Wilson rides a motorbike, which if you are very good, we shall all take a look at during morning break."

A thunderous round of applause broke out, accompanied by a high-pitched hubbub as the children chatted and either pointed or waved at the masked figure as Lyn welcomed Liz Williams to the stage.

"WELL DONE, Liz It's not often we have a visitor who can keep that lot in rapture for half an hour." She gestured for her visitor to enter the office of her secretary, Tina, who offered Liz a broad smile and the offer of a coffee. Lyn's office was next door, linked by an adjoining door, and within a few seconds, the pair were seated on opposite sides of Lyn's paper-strewn desk.

"Thanks for staying back after your talk and letting the children look at the bike. It looks a scary thing to me. Doesn't it scare you at all?"

Liz laughed. "Not one bit. My dad always had motorbikes, so I've been used to riding them since I was a young 'un. They're great for our winding roads and riding across fields when the need arises. I love it."

Lyn shook her head in mock bemusement. "Better you than me. That's all I can say."

A tap on the half-glass door announced coffee as Tina popped two mugs and a plate of digestive biscuits on the desk. "Hmm, my favourite, thanks, Tina."

The secretary smiled at Liz, acknowledging her thanks and quietly closed the door behind her.

"Liz, I have to be honest. The other reason I wanted you to stay on a bit was so I could talk to you about Burt. Or to be more precise, his wife. Did Jennifer mention anything about Burt's health when you saw her?"

Liz placed her mug of coffee back on the desk and stared into its contents for a few seconds. "What can I tell you? She was distraught—and angry. Jennifer mentioned she had been going on at him for ages to sell up, but he wouldn't. I asked why, and Jennifer said Burt's family had fought so hard over the years to keep the mill. She said Burt's health was more important. The mill was of no use without him."

Lyn sipped her drink as she listened intently to what Liz had to say. "And his health?" She noticed Liz smile.

"It's funny you should mention that. I know now why doctors don't tell anyone what they do for a living; everyone they meet wants a free consultation; human nature, I suppose. So yes, she did mention it, but I can't share it, Lyn. Patient confidentiality and all that."

"Oh, sorry, didn't mean to compromise you."

"Don't worry, I'm used to it, but what I can say is that he seemed to be suffering from the same niggles that many men of his age do who work in a dusty environment. Jennifer did mention Burt bottled things up, but then again, that's like most blokes, isn't it?"

"Poor Jennifer, I must try and get back over to see her." Lyn's eyes watered as she spoke.

"That would be a nice touch, Lyn. I can see how much Burt meant to you. Try and get her talking about him because she seemed to be feeling guilty about not pushing the health stuff with him—" Before Liz could finish the sentence, her radio came to life. She lifted the device from its shoulder cradle and spoke, "November Zulu 264. Roger. Five minutes away. Now en route."

It was only then that Lyn noticed Liz was wearing an earpiece. "Sounds urgent, Liz?"

The first responder nodded as she started to make her way to the door. "Always is at this stage; don't know what I'm going to find but need to dash, Lyn, sorry."

A second later, and Liz had left the office. Thirty seconds after that, Lyn heard a throaty roar as Liz brought her motorbike to life.

———

WHAT A STUPID CAR THIS IS.

Lyn sat forlornly behind the wheel of her MINI Clubman and turned the key in the ignition one more time.

Dead as a dodo.

She pressed a hot key on her mobile and lifted the phone to her ear. "Fitch, it's Lyn. I just finished school, and my silly car won't start. Any chance of you having a look?"

"Again? Not to worry, I'll get Rachel to walk over; it'll be a good experience for her."

"Thanks, Fitch, you're a star."

"Two minutes, then."

"Great." Lyn disconnected the call, got out of the car, and peered towards a kink in the road, watching for Rachel. Fitch was as good as his word. Within thirty seconds, the familiar figure of a young girl in a dark blue coverall came into view.

"That was quick. Thanks for popping over, Rachel."

The teenage apprentice smiled, and within seconds had the car bonnet up and was bent over its inner workings.

"Try it now, Lyn, will you?"

Lyn did as she was instructed. "Nothing, I'm afraid."

Rachel reappeared and walked the few feet to where Lyn was sitting.

"I recognise the sound. Come and have a look, and I'll show you what I think is wrong."

Lyn unfolded herself from the driving seat.

Won't have a clue what I'm looking at, but better show willing.

"See that. I reckon that's your problem."

Lyn looked to where Rachel was pointing. All she could see was a mass of pipes and cables. "You think so?"

Give me a clue, Rachel.

She watched as the teenager wrestled with a cable connector buried deep in the bowels of the engine compartment.

"Try that for me will you, Lyn?"

She climbed back into the MINI and once again turned the ignition key, more in hope than expectation. The car sprang into life. "How clever, Rachel, that's fantastic. Thank you so much."

Rachel closed the bonnet and gave Lyn the broadest of smiles. "See, I told you."

Lyn wasn't sure what the girl had said the problem was. Neither did she care. All that mattered was that she once more possessed a working car.

Rachel walked back around to Lyn and spoke to her through the open window. "I've always loved these cars."

Lyn took the hint. "Have a sit in and see what you think." She turned the ignition off, got out, and gestured for the girl to take her place. "Like it?"

Rachel wore a broad smile as she settled herself into the driving seat and turned the engine over. "Listen to the sound of that. Fast too, all to do with the power-to-weight ratio and the gearing, of course."

Lyn's eyes glazed over as she tried to look interested in listening to Rachel in full flow on the technicalities of the car's performance. "I'll take your word for it, Rachel. I just want it to get me from here, there, and back."

The apprentice laughed as she gave the accelerator a final sharp press and delighted at how quickly the engine responded. "Listen to that exhaust. Doesn't it sound fantastic?"

Lyn shook her head. "You might as well be talking Russian, but it seems you have a thing about noisy exhausts."

The girl's smile widened as she listened to Lyn. "Yeh, but only when they're working properly. You should have heard the one I worked on yesterday. Shocking, it was."

Lyn's ears pricked up. "Working on a Sunday?"

"Only when we are extra busy, and Fitch pays a good rate of overtime, so I don't mind."

Lyn smiled again. "Well, that's good to hear. Anyway, did you fix it? The exhaust, I mean."

Lyn's clarification caused Rachel's confused look to dissipate.

"Yep, no problem, though why he left it so long, I don't know. If he'd have come to us a few weeks ago, he'd probably only have needed the back end replacing. As it was, we had to change the lot, so his laziness cost him."

I wonder, could it be our mysterious exhaust man?

"So you know him, then?"

Rachel looked up at Lyn, who was now leaning more deeply into the car from the open door. "Oh, I know him all right. He really fancies himself does Peter Lomas."

TUESDAY EVENING TURNED out to be little different from earlier in the day. The only change was that it was now dark and cold instead of sunny and cold.

"At least it's warm in here. Winter seems to be going on forever," said Lyn as she took her seat for dinner at The Ravens Inn in St. Mary Staith. "Ant, are you listening to me? I said—"

"Only old people talk about long winters, Lyn." He smiled as he sat opposite Lyn in the cozy dining room of the eighteenth-century pub. "I thought you preferred it to hot weather. You moaned enough last summer when we had that heatwave."

She bristled as she picked up a menu and glanced at its contents. "There's the weather, and then there's Norfolk weather. That east wind can still cut you in half, and I prefer to be able to breathe properly instead of sucking bits of air through my teeth. Anyway, I do like the sun; I just don't like being burnt to a crisp. It's not good for a girl's complexion."

Ant raised his eyebrows as he joined Lyn in looking at what was on offer. Meals ordered, the two friends mulled over the case for murdering Burt and their progress to date.

"We don't seem to be very much further on, do we?" Lyn offered to pour Ant a glass of water as she spoke. "It's not as if there aren't enough suspects. As I see things, we've rather too many."

Ant took a sip of the water and pulled a face. "Ugh, tap water. I hate the stuff. Where's my Fen Bodger got to?" He looked over his shoulder towards the bar, relieved to see what looked like their drinks order being prepared. "You can never have too many suspects, Lyn. Our job will be about eliminating rather than trying to find them in the first place."

Lyn's eyes widened. "So, you think one of them did do it?"

His attention wavered for a few seconds as their drinks arrived, and he took the first gulp of his pale ale. "Ah, that's better. Yes, I do."

Ant's two-part response confused Lyn for a few seconds until she realised the latter half had nothing to do with the first bit. "But which one of them, that's the question?"

"No, it's not. The real question is will I get mushy peas or garden peas with my cod?" Ant shimmied to one side as food appeared over his shoulder to be placed expertly in front of him by the waiter. "Just the job, mushy peas."

Lyn hunched her shoulders as her beef Wellington arrived. "You know, for someone who has a title and lives in a place big enough to hold a football match in, you are a pleb."

Fork hanging mid-air loaded with cod, Ant feigned a lofty look. "Man of the people, if you don't mind."

"That's what I said," replied Lyn.

Here we go, Roman history lesson coming up, thought Ant.

"I know that look, Anthony Stanton, so no, I'm not going to explain. Now be quiet and eat your meal."

Yes, mother.

Out of nowhere, a kerfuffle kicked off from the far corner of the room. Men shouted, there was the sound of glass breaking, and women's voices were raised. After a few seconds, Ant decided he'd had enough. He stood and turned in the direction of the row. Two men were pulling at each other over their dining table with what looked like their partners trying to untangle the pair. Ant's army training kicked in.

"Enough, you two. I'm trying to eat my meal as are the

other good folk all around you. Now, if you can't behave, I suggest you leave."

Ant's intervention seemed to stun the antagonists into silence. Now it was so quiet you could have heard a pin drop. Just then another man sped in from a different part of the restaurant. Ant looked around at the approaching man. It was Detective Inspector Riley.

"Well, for once you are doing something useful. Now, what's all this silliness about?" Riley gave each of the men a stern look; neither answered his question. "If you can't behave, leave. If you don't leave, I will arrest you for breach of the Queen's peace." He retrieved his warrant card from his jacket pocket to establish his credentials in the matter. One of the women made as if to interrupt the detective. "And that goes for you ladies as well. Do I make myself clear?"

Within a minute the warring couples had left the pub, and a genteel round of applause had broken out for the establishment's two saviours.

"Good evening, Detective Inspector. I wouldn't have expected to see you here." Ant could see his question had rattled the policeman.

"Don't think us poor coppers can afford to eat with the toffs, then?"

Unusually for Ant, he started to take Riley's bait. Lyn spotted the danger and intervened to broker at least a temporary truce.

"Come on, you two. Let's not go from hero to zero in front of these good people."

Her words were enough to bring Ant to his senses.

"I apologise, Detective Inspector. I was out of order. Can I get you a drink?"

Riley nodded, and as both men approached the bar,

Riley responded, "I suppose I was a little harsh, for which I am sorry. And thank you for your assistance. It could have got a little nasty."

High praise indeed.

As the barman handed over their respective drinks and Riley turned to rejoin his table guests, the goodwill seemed to disappear. "Have you discovered Mr Bampton's murderer yet?"

Barbed looks obliged Lyn to again intervene. "Now, you two, that will do."

Ant looked at Lyn accusingly.

Whose side are you on?

"So, you still think it was an accident, Detective Inspector?"

Clever, Lyn.

Riley exchanged his glare from Ant to Lyn. "Unless either of you has anything to tell me to make me change my mind?"

Ant shot Lyn a sharp look, shaking his head almost imperceptibly.

"No, Detective Inspector, nothing at all."

Well done, girl.

Riley dusted his suit down. "In that case, I shall return to my Dover sole and bid you both good evening." The inspector made for the adoring gaze of his fellow diners as he wove his way through a labyrinth of small round tables and disappeared around a corner.

I'll swing for you one of these days.

Resuming their seats, the two friends got on with eating what was left of their meals. Ant was the first to finish.

"He's right, you know. We've nothing to go on other than a crazy hypothesis involving two men scheming to bump off a man who had been kind enough to show them around his mill." He then noticed that Lyn had a sparkle in her eyes. "What's up with you?"

Lyn placed her knife and fork neatly back onto her plate, indicating she had finished her meal. "Well, I was going to tell you just before Mike Tyson and Muhammad Ali had a go at one another. Rachel knows who the exhaust man is. His name is Lomas."

"Rachel?"

"Yes, the girl that you dumped on Fitch, remember? Well, it turns out she's quite a mechanic; anyway, she recognised the man but had no reason to think anything of it."

Ant's interest grew as he handed his credit card to the waiter, paid the bill, and helped Lyn on with her coat. "Did she give you an address where we can find him?" He watched as Lyn's smile thinned. "Don't tell me she doesn't know. Well, that's a great help, then."

As Ant opened the door of his Morgan for Lyn, she gave him a cold stare. "Listen, Mr Intelligence Officer, you're the one with the secret contacts, who seems to know everything about everyone. That's your job; now shut the door. I'm freezing.

That didn't come out like I meant it to.

The following fifteen minutes were spent mostly in silence as Ant licked his wounds and wondered how best to start up a conversation that wouldn't result in him getting a slap. He needn't have worried. As he rounded a gentle curve that brought the village church into sight, a battery of blue flashing lights gave him all the help he needed.

"What on earth is going on?" He slowed the Morgan to a snail's pace and parked before getting anywhere near the police cars and ambulance. Sauntering to a huddle of uniformed officers, he caught sight of Riley and Reverend Morton. "This looks serious, Lyn."

As he finished speaking, he felt Lyn pull away. "I know, it's not a pleasant sight, is it?"

Lyn stared at Ant. "It's not what it is, it's who."

Ant took a closer look before a police constable began to gesture for the pair to move back.

"Good Lord, it's Albert Sidcup."

9

MORNING COFFEE

Stanton Hall stood majestically in its perfectly manicured lawns and themed gardens divided into sections by ancient hedging. Wednesday morning meant only one thing for Ant: his weekly run around the large estate on his quad bike to check on things and to say hello to as many estate workers as he could.

Bringing the bike to a halt on the gravel drive, he opened the massive oak double entrance doors and strode into the expansive lobby.

"Will you be joining His Lordship and Her Ladyship for coffee in the morning room, sir? I believe the Reverend Morton is present." Michael had been the butler for several years now and had followed in his father's footsteps in the role. His attire was immaculate with a crisp white shirt and tie adorned with the family motto worn beneath a charcoal-grey waistcoat, which fitted his slim figure like a glove.

"Ah, that's handy. I wanted to speak to the vicar."

"Very good, sir. I shall be along shortly to serve your coffee." The butler turned to make his way down to the kitchens.

"No need, Michael. I'll see to it myself. No sense in inter-
rupting your morning just to sling me a coffee cup."

The two men swapped acknowledging nods and went
their separate ways. In Michael's case, this meant disappearing through a jib door in a richly panelled wall as if he'd
vanished into thin air.

"Morning, Mum, Dad. Hello, Vicar. Michael mentioned
you were here."

"Good morning, son, come and give your old mama a
kiss. Reverend Morton had just been telling us all about that
ghastly incident last night. He says you were there?"

As the vicar poured himself a top-up of coffee, he
gestured to Ant."

"Thanks, Reverend, one sugar, no milk, please."

Sauntering over to a long oak buffet table that had stood
on the same spot for centuries, Ant collected his drink and
made his way over to his mother. "How are you feeling
today?" His words were meant as more than a general greeting. He always worried about her state of health and that of
his father.

"Bright as a lark, my darling. Now, where's my kiss?"

Ant leant down to plant the gentlest of kisses on the delicate skin of his mother's cheek. "That's good to hear, Mum."

But it's not the truth.

His father smiled, watching the tenderness with which
his son treated his mother. "Now, do come on, you're
keeping us all waiting. What did you see last night?"

Ant looked at the vicar. "Not much really, by the time
Lyn and I arrived it had all happened. I'm sure the vicar has
much more detail than me." He watched as Morton drank
the last of his coffee and placed it back on the buffet.

"It's the saddest thing. I came across the man earlier in
the day. He seemed lost in his own world. People often are

when they arrive unannounced during the day. I left him for a while and was about to enter the vestry when he asked to speak to me. Naturally, I agreed and took a seat next to him. After a few moments of silence, and without looking at me, he said his life was in tatters because he knew he could not undo what had been done, and that it was now too late."

The earl shuffled in his button-backed leather chair. "What do you think he meant by that. Seems a strange thing to say, don't you think, Vicar? Too late for what, I wonder?"

Morton shook his head. "I don't know. I tried to get the man to explain so that I might help him, but he rather strangely asked if I believed God forgave sinners. As you would expect, I told him that if a person truly repented, then yes, God would forgive them, to which he responded by asking how God would know. It was such a sad conversation, you know. I have seen many distressed people, but his despair went far beyond anything I've seen before."

Ant turned from having poured himself a refill and turned his attention to the vicar. "Did he say anything else?"

Morton gave a heavy sigh. "That's the thing, Anthony. On reflection I think I may have said that God would know, rather too forcefully. What if he misinterpreted me and assumed he needed to carry out some sort of physical act of redemption? So that God would actually see him? I may have inadvertently been responsible for..."

Morton's voice tailed off into silence as he slumped into one of several chairs placed around the open fire.

After a few seconds of silence, Ant spoke. "What, like jumping off your church steeple?"

The reverend didn't answer. Instead, Morton looked unblinkingly into the pile of burning logs, the loud crackle the only thing breaking an otherwise total silence.

"Come on, old chap. No one could think that you were in

any way responsible for that poor man's death." The earl leant forward and just managed to give the vicar's hand a pat of reassurance, which the man did not acknowledge. "I've seen this sort of thing before, you know, during the war; intolerable stress does strange things to some men." As he said the words he looked urgently at his son. "Sorry, Anthony, I did not mean to draw any parallels with you, it's just—"

Reverend Morton looked confused.

"My PTSD diagnosis from the military. That's why I'm back, probably for good. No need to mention anything outside this room, eh, Vicar?"

"Of course, Anthony, I'm so sorry."

"Anyway, we were talking about why Albert Sidcup should have jumped from your roof, Vicar. This is a strange to-do and rather complicates things around Burt's death."

Ant's sudden change of subject eased the tension that had been growing in the room.

"You don't think, you know... that the fellow had anything to do with—"

Ant shrugged. "All I'm saying is that if experience has taught me one thing, it's that nothing is as it first seems. I spoke to him recently, and it didn't go well. Perhaps he was already on the slide, so to speak."

Reverend Morton tapped an arm of his chair with a forefinger. "Well, that awful detective must think there's more to it than suicide. He was asking me questions twenty to the dozen and made it clear he thought I knew more than I was saying."

The elderly earl dunked a chocolate digestive into his coffee, paying too little attention to the problem with soggy biscuits. "Wretched thing all over my trousers. But about this detective, I suppose the world he inhabits is one in which people are always telling him fibs."

Ant couldn't help smiling at the genteel language his father used, made all the more endearing given the earl's distinguished military record. "I can tell you one thing, Riley and you have in common." His father squinted at his son. "You might well look at me like that, but like Riley, it seems you find it impossible to dunk a biscuit without it going all over you. Look at the state of your pants."

Ant winked at his mother, who was giving her husband a stern look for causing yet more laundry. "What do you think, Mum?"

She raised both eyebrows. "Oh, darling, you are such a clumsy man."

"MILLIE JONES, if I have to tell you one more time to leave Pamela Brown's pigtails alone, I'll have you taken back to school right this minute, do you understand?"

The eight-year-old looked suitably chastened as Lyn led a school party of twenty children on a nature walk along Hickham Broad.

"Thank heavens a few of the parents, and you, could spare the time to act as sheepdogs with this lot, Tina. I know you've got a load to do back in the office."

The school secretary smiled as she gathered two little ones into her looking for shelter out of the cool breeze. "It's nice to get out of that office sometimes, Lyn. Anyway, all things considered, they're not behaving too badly."

Lyn huffed and scanned her charges, her gaze darting from one place to another. "Hmm, if you say so, but you need eyes in the back of your head with this lot. Whose idea was the nature walk anyway?" She reacted to Tina's broadening smile. "Don't tell me, it was mine?"

As the minutes passed, the group's progress along the bank of Hickham Broad was no better than a snail's pace as first one child, then another, discovered something new that they just had to share with everyone else. As the leading group, which Lyn was supervising, rounded a gentle curve in the broad, a man wearing a life preserver and stout wellington boots came into sight. Lyn could see that he was studying something in great detail.

"Hello, Stan. I thought it was you. It's not often we see you this far up the broad. Got a bit of a clampdown going on, have we?"

Stan Fleming had held the position of river warden for as long as Lyn could remember. She remembered him telling off Ant and her more than once as young teenagers for causing mischief of one sort or another.

"Well, no, not really, but as it's quiet during the winter months, it means I can get to places to check boat licences I don't get time to cover during the tourist season."

Lyn looked around anxiously, watching for which children were where. She was glad when Tina arrived with two or three young ones. Looking farther down the broad, she could also see three parents bringing up the stragglers.

At least we've still got them all.

"It looks like you've got your hands full, Lyn. Rather you than me. I'll stick to my boats."

Comfortable everyone was accounted for, Lyn turned back to Stan. "Part of the job, but I tell you what, I wouldn't like to have your job, you know, getting hassle dealing with owners who don't have a licence."

Stan turned his attention to a grubby-looking craft that had been moored in a narrow inlet. "What, you mean like this one?" He pointed to a fibreglass vessel that Lyn thought had seen better days.

"Just goes to show there are parts of any job that cause headaches, Stan. Will you be slapping the owner with a fine?"

Stan gave the old craft a further look-over. "That's what I was trying to find out when you came along. The problem is, there's no licence showing, and the boat doesn't have any identifying name or number; most unusual if you ask me."

Lyn had a quick look around the outside of the craft. "As you say, Stan, not a mark. Do you get much of this going on?"

Stan's shoulders sank. "I'm afraid we see more and more of it. Whether it's because people have less money to spend, or they know us wardens have had our numbers cut, so there's not much chance of being caught, I just don't know. I do know it annoys the heck out of me. Costs a fortune to keep these Broads clear, and people not paying their way do not help one bit."

Lyn was quick to notice how agitated the river warden had become. She had hit a raw nerve. All the children had caught up, along with their chaperones. This caused Lyn to worry about the crowd on what was a relatively narrow path right next to the water.

"Now, children." Her tone was enough to bring the throng to order. "While I talk to Mr Fleming, I want you all to go on ahead. Miss Shore will show you where you might... and I mean might, if you are very quiet, see tawny owls nesting. I also want you to listen out for mistle thrushes and notice just how loud they sing."

Instructions given, the group moved off in single file, with the adult helpers walking on the outside to shield the children against the danger of falling into the broad.

She attempted to cheer Stan up. "How long have you been at this now, Stan? You must have seen some changes?"

Stan perked up at being asked to share his memories of the place. "Well, let me see. It'll be thirty-two years this coming March. Cor blimey, that's a long time, innit?"

"Certainly is, Stan."

"And you know the thing that most people find hard to believe?" He didn't wait for Lyn to respond. "Well, it's that the waterways are in far better condition than they have ever been. The summer might mean we're full of tourists mucking about on big hire boats they can't drive, but it does bring in a lot of money. And like I said, it costs a fortune to keep the waterways in good shape." Stan pointed to the near derelict boat in the inlet. "You see what I mean; some of them can't even be bothered to take their rubbish home with them."

Lyn followed where Stan was pointing. The open deck of the small craft was covered in an assortment of bottles, boxes, bits of old wood, and bags of paper. "Any chance of finding who it belongs to, given the boat lacks any identification?"

Stan put a finger to the side of his nose and tapped it. "I'll have a good old rummage through this lot. Sometimes I get lucky, and there's something with a name or an address on it. I've found people more than once like that. You should see the look on their faces when I turn up with a penalty notice that costs them a few bob."

Lyn began to take more interest in the detritus. "Th sounds like fun. I can give you five minutes before I need catch up with my little terrors."

For the next few minutes, Lyn held open a heavy- plastic sack, into which Stan threw all manner of thing not before first scrutinising each piece of paper for potential evidence.

"Look at this stuff, Lyn." Stan uncrumpled paper after paper, holding anything of possible interest out for Lyn to have a look at. "Look, here's an electricity bill. The clever blighters have ripped the account number and personal details off, so you see, they know what they are doing is wrong."

As Stan picked up the next pile of paper, Lyn spotted a flyer. "Well, whoever it all belongs to, they're interested in social history. That's about water and grain mills."

Stan gave the flyer a passing glance as he threw it into the plastic bag with the remainder of the rubbish.

"Well, now, that's done, Stan. I'd better be off, or they'll think I've got lost."

As Lyn waved Stan goodbye, he thanked her for the help as he made off in the opposite direction.

It didn't take her long to locate her charges. She was pleasantly surprised to see the children were listening intently to birdsong, which Tina was busy identifying for 'hem.

"Looks like you've found your vocation, Tina."

The secretary gave Lyn a wry smile. "Er, I don't think so. 'ple of hours is enough, and I'm already missing my 'er and coffee percolator."

'two women laughed as children buzzed all around

you lot. Time to head back to school. Your 'be waiting for you, and we don't want to keep 'do we?"

' "Oh, miss," rang out, but Lyn was having

vone back to the minibus."

Fifteen minutes was all it took to reach their transport. As Lyn was assisting the last of the children into the minibus, she heard the familiar roar of Ant's Morgan pulling up.

"Been to the zoo, then, have we?"

Lyn gave Ant a withering look. "Oh, very funny. You should try keeping twenty boisterous children occupied for a couple of hours some time."

"Like I said, Lyn, the zoo. Anyway, I'm off to see Burt's wife. Not going to be easy, but I'll let you know how I get on." He pressed the car's accelerator and was gone before Lyn had a chance to say anything.

———

"I'M SO SORRY, Jennifer. I know losing Burt has been the most awful shock for you, but I just wanted to bring you a card from all the staff back at the Hall."

The pale-looking widow opened the front door wide so that Ant could pass into the interior of the house. Ant couldn't help but think it looked as though Burt had left for work a few minutes previously. On the hall stand hung a coat Ant had seen Burt wearing many times. On a sideboard, a bunch of keys lay waiting for their master in a brightly decorated ceramic dish. Most difficult of all to make sense of was Burt's packed lunch, still sitting from where he had forgotten to pick it up on Saturday morning. Ant made no comment as he passed through the small space and into the kitchen.

"I know how hard this must be for you. We all miss Burt terribly, but I want you to know that we are all here for you. If there is anything you need, anything at all, just ask."

Ant knew his words would cause Jennifer to break down.

That had not been his intention but he was determined to let the widow know that people cared deeply for her and her daughter.

"Everyone's been so kind. It's hard, but I remember when you lost your brother. You were so brave. Well, for my Sophie's sake, I need to be brave now."

Her words took the wind out of his sails. Ant hadn't expected for a second that amid her own grief, she would be thinking of others. He resisted the temptation to dwell on the memories Jennifer had placed in his head. Now was the time to think about the daughter, and her: no one else.

The second thing he hadn't been prepared for was the extent to which Jennifer wanted to speak about Burt. Never one for many words, a torrent of memories now flowed. Some of these Ant could share from Burt and his time growing up in the village. Others bordered on private matters between man and wife. Still, the memories came. Then as quickly as Jennifer had opened up, she now shut down, and the tears came.

Go on, Jennifer, let it out.

Never useful in such situations, this time Ant felt strangely more at ease. He took it as a sign of his long friendship with Burt and the memories his wife had been brave enough to share.

"Can I get you anything, Jenn?" It was a long time since he had shortened her name and regretted it as soon as he spoke the word, worrying that she might think him overfamiliar. He needn't have worried; if anything, that very familiarity seemed to calm Jennifer down.

"You know, Anthony, I made him go to the doctors, and he did... eventually. But he wouldn't tell me what was said. I've been so worried for him, and now look what has happened."

10

TRUTH OR DARE

The good people of Stanton Parva tended not to bother Dr Thorndike's surgery too much on a Wednesday afternoon. He had always thought it had something to do with a throwback to half-day closing and that the villagers had yet to catch up with modern trends. This meant Ant had no trouble in getting an appointment. However, even then, it involved getting past the formidable Miss Peregrine, the surgery's long-standing receptionist.

Clad in her trademark tweed skirt and jacket, the elderly lady peered over her horn-rimmed spectacles. This made Ant feel as if he was being given the once-over for admittance or ejection from the pristine interior of the half-timbered building.

You always make me feel like a fraud.

"Good afternoon to you, Miss Peregrine. Is the doctor available? I do have an appointment." Ant pondered what her first name might be since no one in the village seemed to know. Waiting for the inevitable inquisition, he prepared himself as best he could.

"Good afternoon, Lord Stanton. You say you have an

appointment? Let me just check that." She had always refused to drop his formal title. Then again, she always insisted on being addressed as Miss Peregrine. "Ah, yes. And may I ask the nature of your symptoms so that I may accurately brief the doctor?"

He instinctively bridled at being asked such a question. Ant knew this was the modern approach. However, in a small village such as Stanton Parva, he couldn't help feeling it gave the tweed-clad lady significant power over her fellow villagers.

Truth or dare?

"The truth is, Miss Peregrine, I have the most awful itch, although I would prefer not to elaborate, if you know what I mean." He watched as the receptionist curled a lip and failed to resist staring at his groin area. "I'm sure you will be used to being told all manner of gruesome details, and it's nothing like that. Nevertheless, the matter is a delicate one, which I am reluctant to expose someone as refined as yourself to."

If Lyn were here, she'd give me what for.

Miss Peregrine moved her ramrod-straight back at an acute angle to put more distance between receptionist and patient. "I see, Lord Stanton. I shall see if Dr Thorndike is available and ensure he is suitably briefed. Now, please use the hand sanitiser and take a seat."

He did as instructed and spent the few minutes it took for the receptionist to return by glancing at the many posters on the wall. These variously advised against smoking, drinking, eating too many cakes and avoiding red meat.

Doesn't leave much to do.

"Anthony"—the clipped voice of Dr Thorndike yanked Ant back from thoughts of all the damage he had obviously done to his body over the years—"do come through."

Thorndike's consulting room was a clone of the thousands of others around the world, with the obligatory bed, various investigatory instruments, and the dreaded weighing machine.

"What's all this nonsense about a personal itch? You've got Miss Peregrine in quite a state. It's a long time since I've seen her blush. Do you think it's anything to do with being near the ruling family, so to speak." The doctor wore a mischievous smile.

Ant reciprocated. "I've been called many things, sometimes with justification, but 'ruling family,' that's a new one on me. More like a cash cow for the government of the day when one of us meets our maker."

Mutual smiles broadened as Thorndike offered his patient a seat. "As my grandfather used to say, you have to earn it to pay it. Oh, how thoughtless of me. Are you able to sit?"

Ant offered Thorndike a wry smile and accepted the offer of a chair. "They say death and taxes are two things none of us can avoid, and I get that. I just wish politicians would stop assuming it's a never-ending money tree. Once the land is sold, it's gone. You don't get to sell again next time they come calling."

Oops, getting too serious.

Thorndike nodded as he took his chair opposite Ant. "Now, why are you really here, Anthony?"

Ant's smile faded as he prepared to explain what he wanted from the doctor. "You know me too well, Dr Thorndike. The thing is, Lyn and I are looking into poor Burt's death. His wife told us she'd made him come and see you recently, but that he wouldn't tell her what you had said. Is there anything—and I know what you're going to say about patient confidentiality—but are you able to at least hint at what was wrong with Burt?"

Dr Thorndike looked at his computer screen, then back to Ant. "You are right about the limitations placed on me by the need for confidentiality. Therefore, I'm afraid I'm not able to say much. Do you think whatever it is might have contributed to his accident?"

Ant looked at his hands as he picked a non-existent nail snag from a finger. "The truth is, I don't know. What I do know is Detective Inspector Riley is intent on closing the case because he's convinced it was a simple, if tragic, accident. But Doctor, what if it wasn't? What if there is more to Burt's death than we currently know. Lyn and I think we owe it to our friend to find out one way or another. Is that such a bad thing?"

Thorndike shook his head. "No... I mean, yes." He paused. "What I mean to say is, of course it's a good thing to want to get at the truth. The problem comes when, and I don't mean to sound offensive, the problem comes when a hunch that something might not be as it seems, cuts across my legal duty. I've already had that Riley fellow around insisting I give him chapter and verse on Mr Bampton. The pompous ass even went as far as to threaten me with a court order to release the man's medical records: such audacity."

The doctor got up from his chair and paced around the small consulting room. Ant could tell the man was in torment.

"I'm sorry, Doctor. I should not have put you in such a compromising position. It's just—"

Thorndike cut in. "I understand, Anthony, and would like to help. It's just... oh, in for a penny, in for a pound. Listen, come back later this afternoon, five o'clock, yes? Miss Peregrine will have left by then, and there's always a ton of medical records left to put back in order. I could do with an extra pair of hands, and I know I can trust you not to look at any when you handle them, yes?"

Clever old Thorndike.

"Of course, Doctor, delighted to help. You say around five?"

The doctor gave Ant a stern look. "I mean at precisely five p.m."

———

THE WATER'S Edge tearooms overlooked Stanton Broad with an uninterrupted view of the water, which stretched out for a good three hundred yards before turning sharply to the right and out of sight. Edged with a variety of oak and fruitwood trees, the broad stretch of water had a grey tinge to it as it lay calm in the fading light of the winter's day.

In the summer, its outside deck area would have been full of customers eating and drinking while looking out for a variety of wildlife. And nervous holidaymakers trying to control their hire boats and avoid grounding their craft in the shallower edges of the broad. The tearoom's exterior looked forlorn as what visitors there were retreated to the cozy interior of the thatched building.

"I just managed to get us in before they closed. Well done for skiving off school early. I suppose that's one advantage of being the head teacher." The pair entered the snug venue, took off their heavy coats, and sat at a small oblong table next to a large picture window, allowing a panoramic view across the broad.

"It's all right me leaving the school early, Ant, but it doesn't mean the work has gone away, you know. It's just more to do later."

He offered Lyn a cheeky grin. "Just imagine a glass of white wine and a plate full of ham, egg, and chips."

"How romantic, Ant, and I hope you haven't brought me here to imagine eating. I'd like to do it for real, please."

As the pair interrogated the menu, a rotund gentleman wearing a white shirt and sober tie approached their table holding a small pad in one hand.

"Are you ready to order?" Thirty seconds later, the man retraced his steps and disappeared into the kitchen before returning to the bar and bringing his two customers their drinks.

"Cheers, Lyn. Enjoy your wine. I don't mind in the least drinking lemonade."

She teased him by grinning broadly and taking a size-able gulp from her wine. "Serves you right for insisting we come in that open-topped freezer of yours. I'm only just thawing out. Anyway, tell me how you got on with Jennifer yesterday?"

As they tucked into their meals, Ant told Lyn about his visit, and in particular about Burt's reluctance to share what the doctor had said to him.

"Well, it matches what Lucy told me about Jennifer's concerns. But it doesn't move us on any, does it? If he didn't tell his wife, then we're stumped. It's not as if Dr Thorndike is going to blab, is it?"

Ant cut a large slice of ham from his plate, dunked it in his egg and completed his next mouthful by adding two chips to his fork. "Well, that's where you are wrong, or at least partly wrong. Yes, you are correct in assuming he won't break the rules on patient confidentiality. Still, he has agreed we can help him put his patient records back in order in"—Ant made an exaggerated gesture in looking at his wristwatch—"precisely twenty-two minutes, so get a move on."

Lyn squinted at Ant through her glass of wine as she took another mouthful. "You do talk rubbish sometimes, you know. Now, what are you blabbing on abo—Oh, I see. You mean—"

He stuffed a mountain of food into his mouth to annoy Lyn. "Indeed I do," or at least that's what he intended to convey. Instead, the result was a combination of potato and words.

"You are disgusting, Anthony Stanton. If your old nanny was about now, she'd have cuffed your ears."

You're not wrong.

The sound of Ant choking brought the man in the white shirt and slim tie back out of the kitchen. "Is sir all right?"

Lyn had already given him a thump on the back far in excess of the force required. "He's fine, and thank you for checking. My friend is just a pig. He's always been a sloppy eater."

The man in the tie relaxed, turned on his heels, and vanished as quickly as he had appeared. "Serves you right, Anthony Stanton, and what a waste of good food."

Her comments forced Ant to view the congealed lump of food, which now sat in a sloppy pyramid just to the side of his plate.

It took Ant several seconds to catch his breath and lose his pallid complexion. "Well, I enjoyed that."

She shook her head. "You are stupid when you put your mind to it. No... correction. You're just stupid."

Acknowledging there was little to be gained by arguing the point with his table companion, Ant looked at his watch again. "Come on, we'd better get a move on, or Thorndike will assume we're not coming and shut up shop."

"I'll shut up shop, you. Are you capable of driving?"

———

PEERING through the sleet hitting the Morgan's narrow windscreen, Ant hit the switch to turn on the wiper blades. "Stupid things are worse than useless. I told Fitch they needed changing."

Lyn was more occupied with keeping the constant drip of water penetrating the fabric roof of the sports car from soaking her left leg to worry too much about what Ant could, or could not see. "When are you going to get a proper car. You know, like the ones normal people drive?"

Ant huffed as he tried not to bite on Lyn's well-aimed insult to the pursuit of mechanical excellence. "This car is a classic, let me tell you. You won't find many left."

Lyn scowled at her friend. "And for good reason. If folk wanted a good soaking when driving, they would buy a motorbike. Now, how much longer have we got before we reach dry land?"

Tempted to fight his corner, he knew there was little point. When Lyn was in this sort of mood, she was as sharp as a tack and would beat him hands down. Instead, he decided to change the subject. "Who in their right minds would jump off a church steeple, Lyn?"

They squinted out of the rapidly steaming-up windows. They looked to their right at the imposing standing of the medieval village church.

"Presumably someone who's been exposed to half an hour in a leaky, draughty tin box with a cloth roof."

Her mood's not improving.

Ant ignored Lyn's caustic comment. "No, seriously. Who does such a thing without anyone suspecting something wrong or seeing what was going on. After all, there would have been a few lads about as the pub emptied out, yet no one saw a thing?"

He looked at Lyn, hoping his serious face would snap her out of her mood. It worked.

"Wait a minute, what about the CCTV Reverend Morton said was being installed. Surely that will show something?"

Ant shook his head. "I doubt it. He said it was on the blink, remember, so that counts that out."

Catching sight of the village surgery, Ant brought the car to a standstill. After waiting a minute or so to see if the sleet abated, the decision was made to make a run to cover the four or five yards from the Morgan into Dr Thorndike's place of work.

"Shocking, isn't it?" Ant appeared to have caught the doctor off guard as the medic stood back up from retrieving a paper file that had fallen to the floor. "The weather, I mean. He noticed the blank stare Thorndike was giving him. "You said I should come back after afternoon surgery to help with the files. I hope you don't mind I've brought Lyn to help out?"

The doctor, at last, gave a look of recognition. "Ah, yes, of course. Now, let me see. Yes, why don't both of you follow me to my consulting rooms."

Ant and Lyn swapped looks and started to chuckle. "And I thought my memory was terrible," said Lyn.

Once inside the clinically clean room, Ant's attention was drawn to two large piles of paper folders stacked on the doctor's stainless-steel-framed desk. "Are these the files you need sorting, Dr Thorndike?"

The doctor picked one pile up and gestured to the second. "I'll take these through. Can you two sort that lot out into alphabetical order? It will make it so much easier to file them away. I shall be gone exactly five minutes. I'm sure by that time you will have somewhere else you need to be. Do we understand each other?"

Not waiting for an answer, Dr Thorndike left the room, not lingering to close the door behind him.

"Am I missing something, Ant?"

He thumbed the top few files. "As you said, Lyn. He is bound by the rules of confidentiality. On the other hand, we are not."

Lyn's face lit up as she caught on.

Subdividing the files into two heaps, Ant pointed at those he wanted Lyn to check. "Remember, Burt's middle name was Richard, so watch out for how the files are labelled, We don't want to miss it in the few minutes we have before Thorndike comes back. Let's not compromise the man any more than we have already."

Two minutes of furious sifting followed as the two friends checked one file, then another.

"Well, look what I've found."

Ant stopped what he was doing to glance over at a file Lyn was holding. "Is it his?"

Lyn opened the file and quickly scanned its contents. Slowly closing the file, she looked over at Ant.

"We can go now, poor Burt."

11

BRUISED KNUCKLES

S trolling across the chequer-patterned tile floor of Stanton Hall's entrance lobby, Ant picked up one of the late edition morning papers from a mahogany table and scanned the headline: "Thunder Thursday."

Just another day in good old Blighty, then.

Passing down a long oak-panelled corridor he passed through a wide doorway into the library, where his father had his head in a book.

"Morning, Dad. How are you this morning?" Ant rested a hand on the old man's shoulder as he passed by and slumped into a leather carver chair opposite his father.

"Tip-top, son. Have you had breakfast? Mrs Smithson did us proud this morning with the kedgeree."

Ant pulled a face as if he were facing his least favourite school lunch.

"Dad, you know I don't like that concoction, but the sausages where top notch, I'll give you that."

His father smiled as he turned a page on the deeply embossed book in front of him. "Just teasing, Anthony, as well you know. Now, tell me what you're up to today."

Lifting the latest copy of *Country Life* from the small table that separated father and son, Ant thumbed through its pages without obvious intent. "I could do with a bit of advice, actually, Dad. There's a couple of things I intend following up on about Burt Bampton's death, and I'm a bit stuck."

The old earl stopped reading and looked at Ant while simultaneously closing the substantial book he'd been engrossed in. "Things must be serious if you're asking me to help, but go on, fire away."

Ant traced an abstract pattern on the glossy front cover of the magazine with a forefinger. "I've just come off the phone from Jennifer, you know, Burt's wife?"

His father nodded.

"I needed to ask her about her husband's health in a little more detail than she mentioned when I saw her recently."

"And?"

"She said he would often be happy and full of energy one minute, then lethargic and quiet the next and sometimes shaking."

Quiet fell for a few seconds, and Ant became aware of his father studying him intently. Eventually, the elderly gentleman spoke.

"Does Mr Bampton remind you of anyone, son?"

Ant glanced at his father before breaking eye contact and leaning back in his chair.

But he ran a grain mill?

"It's no use staring at the table, Anthony, and I know you don't like to talk about your condition, but don't you see, the biggest problem with people similarly afflicted? The inability to discuss their issues?"

The wisdom of his father's words took time to hit home.

"But Burt hadn't been anywhere near a battlefield, Dad. How could he?"

"Anthony, it's not like you to think so narrowly. Post-traumatic stress does what it says on the tin, so to speak. The condition isn't known as shell shock anymore, for good reason. The boffins have come to understand that anyone, at any time in their lives, may experience a traumatic experience that they cannot process, so it stays with them. It festers, until the sufferer can't deal with it anymore, and well, I suppose, shuts down. I guess it's a way of the brain protecting itself. Make sense?"

The son looked at the father.

So wise, Dad.

"I take it you're saying—"

"I'm not saying anything, Anthony. As far as your investigation into whether Mr Bampton's death was an accident or foul play, think more broadly than others; trust your instincts—and military training. Most of all, be interested in the things others are not, and you will find the answer to your question.

It was as if a light bulb had gone off in Ant's head. "Thanks, Dad, you've given me an idea."

Racing down the corridor, he headed for the exquisitely decorated drawing room, thumbed a business phone directory, and lifted the desk phone.

"Is this the Insurance Broker's Guild, London?"

———

"YES, Tina, I'll be back for my meeting with the Richardsons, but I need to get some clothes to the dry cleaners, or

I'll be wearing the same outfit to the next heads' meeting for the third time in a row." Lyn closed the call on her mobile and fumbled with her jacket to put the phone away, while holding an armful of clothes in her other hand.

Stupid things, why don't they make pockets easier to get into?

Eventually she managed the task and pushed the old timber door of Langard's Dry Cleaners open, almost falling forward into the counter as she did so.

"Sorry about that, Sheila, in a bit of a hurry. I hope I haven't broken your door?"

The friendly smile of the proprietor beamed back at Lyn as she began sorting through the various garments Lyn had almost thrown on the countertop. "Not at all, Lyn. That silly door has been biting my customers for as long as I can remember. In fact, I recall father saying he must get it fixed, and he's been dead twenty-seven years."

Lyn paid little attention as she pressed down her dress and rearranged a rain jacket that was still recovering from a heavy shower earlier in the morning. "Pleased to hear that. Sorry I can't stay to chat, I have a pair of disgruntled parents to calm down, and if I'm not back in my office in five minutes, Tina will not be at all best pleased."

"Lyn Blackthorn, you haven't heard a word I said, have you?"

"So, can you have them ready for Friday?" said Lyn as she raised a hand to open the door while looking back at the shop owner.

"Yes, yes, go on, I can see you're all of a lather. See you Friday, around twelvish?"

Within a split second, Lyn let out a loud yelp. "Ow, what the—"

"So sorry, madam, I, oh, it's you."

Lyn scowled at the familiar rumpled figure of Detective

Inspector Riley. "And does the fact it's me make any differ-ence to your clumsiness and bad manners?" Her knuckles were still stinging from the knock they had received as Riley opened the door against them. She glanced at the armful of clothes the detective was carrying. "A dinner suit, special occasion, then?"

Riley was still blushing as he stumbled for words. "Annual policemans' ball."

Although Lyn was still in pain, she couldn't help bursting out in laughter as did Sheila.

"You mean those things really exist? I thought they were just the stuff of comedians' acts." Lyn winked at the shop owner who was thumping the countertop, such was her amusement.

Riley gave the two women a look of indignation. "I'll have you know ours are bigger than that of Thetford and Kings Lyn divisions combined."

Sheila let out another loud roar of laughter as she bent over the countertop and almost banged her head on the wood surface. Lyn's eyes were streaming as tears of laughter ran like a giddy stream down her cheeks. The more indig-nant Riley looked, the more the women laughed.

"What do you mean, Detective Inspector?"

Riley scowled at Lyn. "I simply mean that our balls are bigger than—" He suddenly realised the clumsiness of his diction. "Your response borders on being sexist."

Riley's expression was enough to provoke yet another bout of laughter from Sheila and Lyn.

"Priceless", squealed the proprietor, now completely incapable of stopping her shoulders from raising and lower-ing. Lyn shook her head at the hapless policeman and dabbed the tears away from her face.

"Enough of this nonsense. I should like my suit ready for

collection on Friday. Is that possible? I have no wish to attend the ball in a crumpled garment."

It was all Sheila could do to point at the counter, onto which Riley threw his clothes. Meanwhile Lyn decided she should leave before Tina called to remind her the Richardsons were waiting. As she opened the troublesome door, the dulcet tone of the detective hit home like a knock on the back of her head.

"By the way, perhaps your boyfriend and you may be interested to know that we are now satisfied that the unfortunate Mr Bampton died as a result of a tragic accident. Therefore, there is no need for your partner in crime and you, Tweedledee and Tweedledum, if I may draw the comparison, to waste any more of my time."

Lyn rounded on the detective then thought better of sounding off. Instead she parried with a calm and controlled voice. "Thank you, Detective Inspector. I shall be sure to let poor Burt's wife know what you have just said word for word." She lingered just long enough to see Riley's smug expression turn to panic. Not waiting for a response, Lyn closed the door as best she could and gave him one last glare through the dust-covered door glass. He had started for the door; Lyn didn't wait for her antagoniser.

A few seconds later her mobile rang. Assuming it was the school secretary she at first ignored the call since she would be back in her office in less than sixty seconds. The ring stopped then recommenced. This time Lyn retrieved the mobile from her pocket and looked at the screen. She recognised the number. "Hi, Ant. Listen, I can't talk now; I've got to get back to school. Can't it wait?"

The line went quiet as Lyn walked at pace past the heavy iron-pole fence that lined the pavement boundary of the schoolyard.

"My contacts traced a number for Peter Lomas from the partial number plate we got from Fitch. Can you ring him this afternoon on some pretext or other and see what he knows about Burt?"

Lyn's head was in a whirl as she prepared for her meeting with Alice Richardson's parents and tried to take in the torrent of information Ant was throwing at her. "What am I supposed to say to him?" Her words began to echo as she entered the Victorian stone entrance to the small reception area.

"You'll think of something. Got to go, I need to follow up on a couple of things. Catch up later, yes?"

She didn't wait for Ant to end the call. A harassed-looking Tina stood with folded arms at the entrance to her office. "Thank heavens you're back. I'd have chucked these two out if you'd have been much longer. Good luck."

———

"HERE, I think you deserve a little treat for putting up with the Richardsons. I honestly don't know how you keep your patience." Tina placed a mug of coffee and treat onto Lyn's desk.

"Yum, yum, a chocolate eclair. I always say the sign of a good secretary is anticipating what's coming and making her boss' life easier, and believe you me, just at this moment, chocolate fills the bill."

Tina wore a triumphant smile, blew over two fingers, and made to shine an imaginary set of medals on her chest. "I heard him yelling; was it really that bad?"

Lyn shrugged her shoulders. "Happened before and it will happen again. All my parents think their children are little angels, and I suppose that's a good sign of a loving family. But as we both know, Tina, the reality is far from the idyllic image they have of their little dears." She let out a little giggle as she bit into the eclair. "Hmm, that's delicious."

"Well, I don't want to ruin your moment of bliss, but to remind you, there's a curriculum planning meeting in ten minutes. Don't forget you are chairing it, and you know what a stickler Morgana is for starting bang on time."

Lyn looked forlornly at the remnants of her treat and three-quarters-full mug of coffee. She thought for a moment. "Listen, Tina, can you get my deputy to take it? I want half an hour to catch my breath and catch up on a couple of things."

The secretary attempted a salute. "I'll fix. I'll also keep everything else away from you for a bit."

"Thank you," Lyn mouthed as she picked up the eclair and finished it off in one blissful mouthful.

———

JUST MY LUCK, no answer.

Lyn huffed as she waited for Peter Lomas to pick up the phone. Having worked out a plan of action, she now wanted to get on with it. After attempting to connect several times, she decided to let the mobile go through to answerphone and leave a message.

"Good afternoon, Mr Lomas. My name is Deborah Ickworth, and I'm ringing to congratulate you on winning a valuable prize for being the owner of the thousandth car to be fixed at Fitch's Automotive Services. Perhaps you can ring me back on this number so that I may arrange to get your prize to you. Congratulations again, and I look forward to speaking to you."

Realising she had to work fast, Lyn called out to Tina. Opening the connecting door between their two offices, Tina's head appeared.

"Listen, I know this sounds odd, but when this number rings back, don't announce it, put it straight through to me, okay?" Lyn held out a piece of paper from her notepad.

"Sounds a bit cloak and dagger, Lyn. What are you up to?" The secretary walked the couple of yards over to Lyn and retrieved the paper scrap. "Who is it?"

Lyn smiled and tapped the side of her nose with a finger. "Let's just say I'm hoping it's the greediest man in Norfolk."

Tina looked at the number again then back to Lyn. "If you say so, boss."

Lyn had been correct to think it wouldn't be long before Lomas rang back. Seconds after Tina closed the door, the office phone rang. Lyn tensed and waited until it had rung three times, all the time praying that Tina would break the habit of her work routine and leave the phone for Lyn to pick up.

"Thank you for reaching out to G R & Edy Market Research. This is Deborah speaking, how may I assist you today?"

She held her breath hoping Lomas' greed would get the better of any attempt on his part to validate the call. It worked.

"Uh, yeah. You called me before saying I won a prize. What is it, then?"

"Mr Lomas... may I call you Peter? Well, as I said when I left my message, you are the—"

"Yeah, you told me, but how did you get my number, and how do you know my first name?"

Lyn began to panic. What if he slammed the phone

down? What if he rang back, and Tina picked it up and announced herself with her normal school message?

She had an idea. "Of course, Peter. You are right to be suspicious of calls claiming to offer you a cash prize but let me just ask you this. Did you visit Fitch's Automotive Services on Sunday?"

There was a moment's hesitation.

"Yeah."

"And did you have your car exhaust replaced?"

"Er, yeah, but—"

"Well, Peter, how could we know these things if our offer of a grand prize was a prank? However, I do understand, and if you prefer to decline the prize, I quite—"

"I never said that, did I?"

Lyn allowed the call to fall silent for a few seconds.

"You still there?"

She allowed a further few seconds to pass. "Yes, Peter, I was just looking up the next customer that the garage had on that day, so I'll tell them the good news about the one-thousand pounds, should I?"

"No you won't. One thous... listen, that's my prize; you said so."

Lyn had to stifle a laugh. She was now enjoying the ploy. "Can I take it you are accepting our superb prize after all?"

There was no hesitation this time. "Suppose so. How do I get it, then? I have to stay local 'cos I've got something important on tonight."

Lyn hadn't thought through that bit of her plan. Her mind raced. "Well..." she began hesitantly, "I suppose I could deliver it to you personally. Do you live in the village, because it will be a bit of a run for me?"

Her question spooked Lomas. "Don't matter where I live, but I can meet you by the green?"

So you do know the area.

"Do you know where the buttercross is?"

"Of course I do. I can be there at eight o'clock."

Lyn smiled in triumph.

Yes.

"That's wonderful. I'll see you at eight sharp, then. Goodbye for now, Peter."

Lyn finished the call to stop Lomas asking any further questions.

Greed is indeed a powerful thing.

"ARE you sure this will work, Ant?"

Lyn looked concerned as she turned to Ant as the Morgan approached the centre of Stanton Parva.

"No guarantees, Lyn. But my gut feeling tells me the lure of something for nothing will get him to come. From what you told me, he didn't even ask what his prize was, did he?"

His answer made Lyn think. "Yes, you're right, how can people be so stupid?"

Ant laughed. "For the same reason thousands of people around the world get scammed every day. On the whole, people believe what they're being told, especially when it comes to getting something for nothing. All you did, expertly, was to tap into the bit of his brain that controls emotions. You gave him something that he liked, so reason went out the window. I can see I'm going to have to be careful with you from now on. You have skills I didn't know you possessed."

Lyn gave a throaty laugh. "I'm a woman. Beware."

Ant offered Lyn a resigned nod as he slowed the Morgan down to a snail's pace and parked it well away from the buttercross. Engine and lights extinguished, the car blended into its background perfectly.

"Look, he's already arrived. Now just keep him talking while I make my way around from the left. With a bit of luck, he won't see me until it's too late."

Feeling nervous, Lyn nevertheless did as Ant asked and climbed out of the Morgan and began walking. The hundred yards or so felt like a marathon as she slowly neared the ancient cross and confirmed to herself that the hunched figure leaning against the ancient stone monolith was, indeed, Lomas.

"Hi, Peter, a bit cloak and dagger, isn't it? Feels like an Ian Fleming movie."

Lomas gave Lyn a confused glance. "Ian who? Never heard of him."

Lyn realised she needed to keep things a great deal lighter. If she was to keep him occupied until Ant arrived. "Oh, never mind, it's just me showing my age." She giggled in a deliberate attempt to give Lomas the impression he was dealing with a dizzy female.

"Where's my prize, then?" Lyn could tell Lomas was getting jumpy. She reached into an inside pocket of her heavy coat as if to retrieve something, all the time willing Ant to show up before the game was up.

What if he wallops me?

Lyn decided on a high-risk strategy and began to talk about Burt Bampton's death. She knew he might take flight, but she had no choice.

"Why you talking about 'im? Just some old bloke who fell down the stairs, yeah?"

Lyn's mind began to race again.

Where are you, Ant?

"Well, that's what everyone is saying, but I heard a

copper in the cake shop at lunchtime, and he said they think there's more to it. Have you heard anything?"

Lyn realised she'd spooked him.

"Wait a minute, when you rang me you said it was a long run for you to get here, so how come you were already in the village when you rang me? What's your game?"

Lyn realised she was showing genuine fear but couldn't stop the obvious signs.

He's going to hit me. Where are you, Anthony?

Lomas made as if to raise his hand to her. Lyn waited for the blow to land. Nothing. She opened one eye to see what was happening, only to see Lomas sprinting into the night at a tremendous pace.

Next, she heard the unmistakable sound of Ant's Morgan thundering past with its lights still extinguished.

Great, you big lump. Now I'm stuck on my own.

Less than two minutes later she picked up on the low rumbling of a car as the Morgan slowly reversed to where Lyn was standing.

"I suppose you lost him, and why didn't you do what you said you were going to do? I thought he was going to attack me."

Ant gave Lyn a sheepish look. "You seemed to be doing so well, I thought I could afford to hang back then come steaming in like the cavalry."

Lyn's look of annoyance intensified. "I'll give you cavalry. I suppose you lost him?"

Ant's face dropped. "Sorry, yes, he was moving at a heck of a pace, and by the time I stopped the Morgan to give chase, he'd disappeared.

Lyn opened the passenger side door of the Morgan and slumped into the seat. "So now what do we do?"

As she spoke, Ant's phone pinged. When he didn't

answer, she glanced over to see him looking excitedly at the screen.

"Well?"

"My mate at GCHQ has come up trumps. He's given me Lomas' address."

12

THE HOSPITAL

"Why didn't you tell me when we were together yesterday or at breakfast this morning, Dad?"

Ant dropped himself into a hard-backed chair in the reception area of Waverley Cottage Hospital as the men waited for the consultant to call them into his office.

"Well, you seemed pretty low yesterday, and anyway, it was a routine appointment that's been scheduled for weeks. A few minutes after we arrived, your mum—"

"How are you this morning, Your Lordship? Hello, Lord Stanton. Please, both of you, will you join me in my office?" The tall, slim consultant gestured with an outstretched hand. The specialist cut a dashing figure in his dark pinstriped suit and greying hair that had been immaculately trimmed. "Please, do take a seat."

Father and son complied and sat to one side of a computer screen as the consultant pored over a scan.

"Should I be worried, Mr Prentice?"

The consultant sat back in his leather swivel chair and moved direction with his feet so that he was seated face on with the earl. "The good news is that it hasn't got any worse."

"And the bad?"

"Less good, rather than bad, Your Lordship. Her Lady-ship's condition is such that from time to time, she will relapse, particularly if she overdoes things."

The earl's demeanour lightened. "Ah, I see. However, you know what she's like, never has come to terms she's in her seventies Do you know, she still refers to others in her circle as 'old,' without ever considering she is the same age as most of them."

Prentice smiled as he took another brief look at the scan. "I know what you mean; my mother is exactly the same. Nevertheless, things will have to change. You observed what happened earlier. My concern is that while the condition itself won't—how should I put this, may not see her off, it may be that the next time, it won't be something quite so forgiving as one of my nurses' outstretched arms your wife falls into."

The earl nodded as he listened. His son was less convinced. "Do we need to be a little more insistent with Mum?"

His father began to chortle. "Good luck with that, son. Are you going to tell your mother? Because I'm not. With age comes wisdom; with common sense comes a boxing of the ears. Will you risk yours?"

Prentice laughed as father and son traded the relative merits of requiring hearing aids as a reward for offering advice to wife and mother.

"So," began the consultant, "my advice is we keep her in for a few days' observation and to get her stabilised. As for future action, I leave that difficult matter in the hands of you two worthy gentlemen."

Leaving the consultant's office, the earl turned towards

his son. "Not a word to your mother, then?" The old man's eyes twinkled as he made his point.

"So be it, Dad. We'll just have to keep a closer watch over Mum, without her catching on."

The earl laughed as he made for his wife's room. "Good luck with that too. Now, what have you on for the rest of the day? Better you don't come through because your mother will only think we're up to something if she sees us together."

Ant studied his father's demeanour. He may have sounded jovial enough, but the son knew when to back off. "I thought I'd drop in on Lyn. There's a couple of things I want to discuss with her. After that, well, we'll see."

His father gave him a pat on the shoulder and began to make off. "Oh, I wonder if you could do me a favour? Could you ask if Lyn would bake your mother's favourite for the weekend? We do so look forward to her cakes."

Ant returned his father's touch of affection. "One Victoria sponge coming up, Dad."

As Ant neared the exit doors of the cottage hospital, he caught sight of a friend. "Morning, Robin, just the man. I want to pick your brain."

Dr Robin Solomon looked every part the junior doctor as he greeted his old friend. "Good to see you, Ant. What are you doing here, nothing serious I trust?"

Ant explained his presence then turned the conversation to Burt Bampton.

"...Type-two diabetes, you say. The problem with the condition is that so many sufferers don't take their condition seriously. In fact, many people don't know they have diabetes in the first place but left untreated or poorly managed, diabetes can have devastating consequences.

"So, you are saying..."

"Is she who must be obeyed in her den?"

"I heard that, Anthony Stanton, and if you want a cup of coffee and one of Tina's marzipan fancies, you'd better behave."

The school secretary smiled as she curled a finger to call Ant into her office, then pointed at the open connecting door where Lyn was seated.

"How do you put up with her?"

Tina's smile broadened. "It's only you that brings the worst out in our head teacher. Now, do you want that coffee or not?"

"And the fancy?"

"Don't push your luck."

He didn't. Instead, he sauntered the few yards into Lyn's office and sat himself down opposite his most trusted friend. "How's life in the rarefied world of academia, then?"

Lyn opened her arms in a sweeping fashion across heaps of files, journals, and paperwork strewn over her large wooden desk. "As you can see, just another light day in the office. Can I tempt you with a two-thousand-word report to be written on the subject of resource shortages in primary schools? Or perhaps the several hours it will take to update the school's risk assessment policies in readiness for our next Ofsted inspection?"

Ant looked at the untidy mess. "Thank you, but I think I'll settle for the coffee and cake, speaking of which, I have a request from my father."

Lyn held up a finger as if she were silencing an unruly pupil. "Don't tell me, a Black Forest gateau?"

"Wrong. Victoria sponge."

Lyn's smile faded a little. "That's your mum's favourite. Is she okay?"

Nothing gets past you.

Ant briefed her on his hospital visit.

"Be sure to give her my love, and don't forget this time, sieve brain."

He didn't bite based on what happened the last time. "Yes, of course I will. Now, I've got something to tell you."

"Is that the coffee and fancies have arrived?" The voice from behind belonged to Tina as she delivered the late-morning snack. Closing the door behind her, it left the two friends looking at their treat in wonder.

"She really is a great baker. Try this one." Lyn picked up a pink delight and held it to Ant's lips. He didn't hesitate in eating half of the dainty offering in one go while relieving Lyn of the remainder.

"What, better than you?" he mumbled with a mouthful of sponge and marzipan."

Lyn grimaced. "Watch it, you. Anyway, what's so urgent that it can't wait until school's out?"

Finishing his cake and eyeing up a second, Ant told Lyn about his meeting with the junior doctor.

"So you're saying poor Burt may simply have had a funny turn that cost him his life? Lyn played around with some crumbs left on her plate. "It just sounds so unlikely, don't you agree?"

Ant raised his eyebrows. "Not according to my mate, and he's to be believed about people not taking the condition seriously. It's exactly what could have happened. Think about it, Lyn: if Burt wouldn't tell Jennifer what was wrong with him, perhaps he couldn't admit it to himself and carried on as if what he ate and drank, and when, didn't matter."

Lyn blew across the top of her coffee cup before taking an exploratory sip. "But if that's true, then Riley's got it right, and we've been running around annoying folks for the best part of a week; what a waste of time." She stared into her coffee cup and fell silent.

Ant bridled. "I don't define trying to find out the truth of how a good friend dropped dead a waste of time, Lyn. What's up with you?"

His harsh words shocked Lyn. "Don't shout at me. You're the one that said something was, how did you put it, gnawing away at you. You were the one that chased me off to Ron Busby's and nearly got me assaulted. And to top it all off, you were the one that set me up with Lomas and changed your mind about the cavalry charge, remember?"

The pair glared at each other. So loud had Lyn's protest become that Tina half opened the connecting door and popped her head through. "If you two are having one of your domestics, could you do it more quietly. I'm in the middle of putting a plaster on Freddy Simpson's knee again. I don't think you two shouting is doing his feeling of well-being any good at all." With that, Tina quietly closed the door.

The silence which followed gave both friends a chance to calm down. They had a well-worn routine for de-escalating tensions when things kicked off.

"Anyway, you were quite safe at the buttercross. I saw Phyllis and Betty coming out of the chip shop. They would have had Lomas' guts for garters if he'd come anywhere near you."

"So let's get this straight. A wallop from Lomas, or ear bashing from Phyllis for putting myself at risk? That makes all the difference, then."

A few seconds of silence fell as the pair gradually regained eye contact. Then the laughing began.

"That'll cost you dinner, Anthony Stanton."

He feigned disappointment. "Only if I can choose the wine?"

Lyn pondered his request for a second or two. "It's a deal. Now, what's next? Do we call it a day on Burt's death, or have you a cunning plan?"

Ant's grin widened. "Funny you should say that. I'm making plans to confront Lomas, but I need to check a few things out before I give you the details. What I need you to do is go back to visit Jennifer and see if you can find any of the medication that Burt was prescribed. By checking the prescription date and dose against what's left in the packets, we can work out if he was taking his medication correctly. That, at the very least, will tell us if his condition was being managed correctly. Then I think we should pay the vicar a visit; I'll tell you why later. What do you think?"

Lyn looked bewildered. "Heck, where did all that come from, Anthony Stanton? Someone's had his thinking cap on. Okay. I'll call in on Jennifer after school and wait until you deign to give me more information on the other stuff."

Ant pushed his chair back, gave Lyn a thumbs-up sign, and made his way to the outer office.

"You two made it up, then?" Tina wore a broad smile as she interrogated him.

He winked. "You know how it is."

"I know how people who care for each other behave." She looked first at Ant then through the open door at Lyn. Both were smiling.

"SOPHIE HAS JUST NIPPED around to her best friend's house. I guess Instagram isn't enough sometimes, even for teenagers; still, the company will do her good after the week we've had."

Lyn detected a more upbeat tone from Jennifer. However, she knew her emotions were all over the place, and it would only be a matter of time before the pain set in again.

I hope I don't put a downer on things.

"It's good of you to see me, Jen. How are you doing?"

The widow gave Lyn a wistful look and shrugged her shoulders.

"You know how it goes."

Lyn didn't pick up on Jennifer's comment; she knew there was nothing more to say. "Listen, Jen, I have some news about Burt's health. Please don't ask me how I came by it, but I need your help to check something out."

Jennifer frowned as she led the way into the spacious kitchen. "What do you mean?" Her voice sounded defensive.

Lyn knew she had to go for it. "Burt had type-two diabetes. He—"

"He had what?" Jennifer exclaimed.

"I know it's a lot to take in, and please, as I said, don't ask me how I found out, but you can be certain I'm telling you the truth."

The room fell silent as Lyn waited for her news to sink in. Jennifer slowly began to react as she looked intently, though with no purpose, at the tiled floor. "I suppose... I mean, that would explain... so that's why the stupid man was tired one minute then full of energy the next. You know, I wondered why he began to insist we had our meals at the same time. Burt said it was because he wanted us to be together as a family. I thought it strange, but you know how Burt is... I mean... I mean was?"

Lyn closed the few feet between them and put an arm around her friend's shoulder. "I know, Jen. I know."

A short silence followed before Jennifer stirred. "You said you needed my help. What did you mean?"

Lyn took a deep breath. "I know what medication he was prescribed and what Burt should have taken each day. I need to find those tablets to work out if he had been taking them."

Jennifer looked confused as she looked towards a kitchen cupboard. "I told you the other day, Lyn. He wouldn't tell me anything, and I've already checked where we keep all our medication. There's nothing out of the ordinary there." Jennifer released herself from Lyn's loose embrace and walked over to the wall cupboard. Retrieving a tin first-aid box, she lifted the lid. "See, just the usual stuff, so if Burt hadn't kept them here, I don't know where he would have put them."

Just then, Jennifer's daughter sauntered through the open back door. "Who putting what, where?"

At first, Jennifer tried to change the subject. Lyn took a bolder approach. "Your dad, we think he got some tablets from the doctor, but we can't find them, can we, Jen?"

Referencing the mother was a deliberate strategy on Lyn's part if she was to get buy-in from the daughter.

"They'll be in his secret box," replied the young teenager as she walked through to the lounge as if her information was uncontroversial.

The two women looked at each other in surprise before Jennifer called her daughter back into the kitchen. "What do you mean, secret box? What box? Where is it?"

The girl gave her mother a puzzled look. "You mean, you

don't know? Dad thought he was clever, but I've known where it is for years. I can even open it for you if you want?"

That's kids for you.

Lyn didn't wait for the girl's mother to respond. "Absolutely fab. Go on, then."

Sophie led the way out of the back door and through the rear door of a double garage. Once inside, she pointed to what looked like a mangle of discarded wood teeth from the gearing machinery at the mill, rusted barrel hoops, and a faded hemp sack.

"Where?" asked the girl's mother.

Sophie sighed as she peeled the sack back to reveal an old wooden box with the words "Ammunition" stencilled on it.

Jennifer drained of colour. "That was his dad's from the war; he was in the Home Guard. I told Burt years ago to get rid of it. He told me he had. It's full of bullets. Come away, Sophie, that box is dangerous."

Lyn wore a startled look as she watched a smiling Sophie reach up to a high shelf and retrieve a rusty key.

"No it isn't. It's full of rubbish, which I don't know why Dad kept."

The girl's mother looked horrified. "You mean you've been in it before?"

Sophie gave her mum a cheeky smile.

Lyn tried not to laugh at what she knew to be typical child behaviour.

In seconds, Sophie had the box opened, then stepped back. "They weren't there the other week. What are they?"

Lyn moved forward and retrieved four boxes of tablets. "Oh, your dad had a bit of a tummy upset, and the doctor prescribed him some antibiotics, that's all."

Satisfied with Lyn's answer, the young girl sauntered back out of the garage leaving the two women to investigate their contents. "Well, at least we know Burt was doing what the doctor told him; look at the prescription date,"

Jennifer complied then totalled up the remaining tablets. "At least my silly man did as he was told for once. But why didn't he tell me? That's what hurts so much."

Tears began to flow as Jennifer crumpled back against an untidy workbench.

Lyn watched, unable to offer much other than a sympathetic cuddle. After a few moments, the widow began to compose herself and asked Lyn if she wanted a drink.

"Thanks, Jen, but I need to get going. Come on. Let's put this lot back and get you into the house." Lyn placed an assortment of tablets back into their respective boxes and went to place them back into the stout box. As she did so, a piece of paper fell to the floor. Scooping it up, Lyn was about to place it back in the box when she glanced at its contents. "Jen, do you know who sent this? It's unsigned, and there's no address."

Jennifer gave Lyn a perplexed look as she took hold of the note and read its contents. Oh, it's just another one of those people trying to buy the mill off us. We get them regularly. Some were a right nuisance."

Lyn took the note back and studied the neat hand in which it was written. "Seems a bit rude, don't you think? The contents, I mean?" Lyn could see Jennifer was in no mood to engage. "Listen, do you mind if I hang on to this?"

13

DANGEROUS ENCOUNTER

W*here are you? Pick up the phone, silly man.*
Lyn rang Ant's mobile three times before waiting on the line long enough to leave a message. "I have something I need to tell you and think I know who might be behind Burt's death. Ring me back as soon as you get this."

She knew he would be mad at her for striking out on her own to follow what could turn out to be a dangerous hunch, but she'd come to the conclusion she needed to act fast.

Slipping the Mini into first gear, she pulled gently away from Jennifer's house, heading to Ron Busby's Electrical Supplies business.

At least there should be other people about if he kicks off again.

The drive to Lynthorp was a pleasant enough one to keep Lyn's mind off the reception she thought Busby might give her, at least in the main. As she glanced at the meandering broad that the road crisscrossed, she smiled at the one or two brave souls who were aboard their boats contending with a stiffening breeze.

Definitely not tourists.

Heading north, she passed Stalham, then on to North Walsham before turning west towards Blickling. A further fifteen-minute drive found her on a small commercial centre made possible through the conversion of a range of old farm buildings. She was disappointed to notice that besides her own car, only two or three others were parked nearby.

Too late to turn back now.

As she gently closed the car door, her mobile rang. "About time too, Ant. Where have you been all this time?"

"I told you, putting plans in place to tie young Mr Lomas down. He's a slippery character, let me tell you, but I think I've just about got it sorted. Now, where are you?"

Lyn explained her plan. Ant exploded.

"What? After the reception you got last time. Are you crazy? What have I told you about putting yourself in danger, especially when there's no need? Why couldn't it have waited until we could have seen him together?"

Lyn struggled to give a coherent answer. She knew he was right. At the same time, she wanted to show him she had ideas of her own. "Well, it's too late now. I'm here, I'll—"

"It's not too late. I assume you can get back into your car and leave without Busby ever knowing you were there. Well?"

Lyn thought for a few seconds and decided he was right. Perhaps it could wait, except she then heard two men's voices. She turned. One of the men was Busby and he had seen her. "Well, er, actually, Ant, it is too late. He's just seen me." She terminated the call before Ant could come back at her. She could imagine what he'd have said. As she put on a broad smile and strolled confidently towards Busby and the other man, her mobile rang again. Lyn knew who it would be and decided to shut the mobile down.

Come on, Lyn, the more confident you look, the further it will get you.

"Ah, Lyn, so nice to see you again. What brings you all the way out here?"

Busby's friendly tone threw her completely off guard. What was he up to? Was he really that much of a Jekyll and Hyde character?

What on earth is going on?

Then it made sense. The other man was the joker from the Windy Wanderers, the one who always had a sarky comment to throw out from the back of the group. Never had she been so pleased to see another human being.

Busby is either a schizophrenic or just keeping up appearances in front of the man.

"Hi, lovely to see you two. It's Tim, isn't it?"

The man next to Busby smiled and nodded. "You've got a talent for names, I see."

Lyn smiled, trying to hide her nerves. "Comes with the job, I'm a teacher."

Busby's jovial mood continued. "Lyn is modest, Tim. You might remember she is the head teacher of the village school in Stanton Parva. Now, Lyn, why don't you come in, Tim was just leaving, so we can have a nice quiet chat like we did the other day."

The words sent a chill down her spine. If she now knew one thing, it was that she didn't want to spend even one second on her own with the man.

Got to keep you out here.

She thought on her feet. "Oh, sorry, haven't got time. I was just passing on my way to meet a friend at Blickling Hall before it closes for the day. It's ages since I've visited the place, and I feel the need for a dose of Tudor and Jacobite history."

"Then why are you here, Lyn?"

Busby's sudden change of tone reminded her how quickly his mood could change. This wasn't the time to hang around, even with a third person present. After all, she didn't know Tim; she'd only met him once.

"To kill two birds with one stone, so to speak." Her use of the word, kill, was a self-inflicted hit as she wobbled for a nanosecond. "That's to say there's something I want to show you: show you both that I need your help with."

Lyn could see she had sparked Busby's attention. By contrast, Tim seemed baffled by the tension between his friend and the head teacher.

"I have a note... I mean someone gave me a letter, and I wondered if you would be so kind as to see if you recognise the handwriting?"

Tim looked surprised. "A handwritten letter, now that's a novelty these days."

Busby remained silent; instead, watching Lyn's every move as she felt in her pocket for the single piece of paper.

"Bit odd, isn't it? No signature or address for which it was sent. And where's the envelope?" Tim scanned the writing as he questioned Lyn."

"Here, let me have a look at it." Busby relieved Tim of the note and seemed to digest every word.

Lyn decided it was now or never but took the precaution of having her car keys at the ready and had already opened the driver's door a few inches. She watched both men to see if their body language changed. Was Busby's hand shaking as he held the paper, or was she imagining it?

"Nope, can't say I recognise the handwriting," said Busby, his eyes still fixed on the text.

"Give it here and let me have another look." Tim gently took the note from Busby and glanced at its contents again.

"Do you know, I could convince myself that the hand looks familiar. Then again, I suppose anyone could have written it. Tell you what though. Whoever they are, they're rude. The tone of the thing is awful."

Lyn looked back at Busby as she held a hand out to recover the note and place it back in her pocket. Busby's eyes burned into her, and his smile had vanished. Deciding not to push her luck, Lyn settled herself into the driving seat, slammed shut the door, and immediately activated the vehicle's central locking. Winding the window down just enough to make herself heard, Lyn said her goodbyes. "Thanks so much for your help. See you both again soon, I hope."

Busby continued to glare at Lyn as she manoeuvred the car out of its parking space.

He really does give me the creeps.

Driving more recklessly than she typically travelled, Lyn put as much distance between herself and Ron Busby as was possible to do within the bounds of the law. Activating her voice-controlled contacts list, she waited for Ant to answer her call.

"Don't ever switch your phone off again, Lyn. Do you hear me?"

She'd expected the rebuke. Her intention had only been to disconnect Ant's earlier call, not shut the phone down, but in the stress of the moment had made a mistake. She attempted to explain. He was having none of it.

"A mistake like that could cost you dearly, Lyn. It's not a game we're playing, you know." The line fell silent for a few seconds. "Anyway, the thing is you are safe now. Are you okay?"

Lyn's emotions bounced between relief at having got away from Busby, and anger at the way Ant had spoken to her even if she knew he was right. "Ye... yes, I'm fine now. To be honest, I just want to get back home and chill for the rest of the day. The thing is, I still can't get over how quickly Busby changes. You should have seen him. Nice as pie one minute, then the next I get the coldest stare you ever saw."

"If I understand you correctly, Lyn, I have seen that look before and let me tell you, you were lucky that the other bloke was there. If Busby had got you into his office, I..."

He fell silent. It brought home to Lyn just how stupid she had been. "Can we talk about something else, please, like that meal you promised me for almost getting attacked —again."

She could hear him chortling down the phone.

"Don't forget we're off to see the vicar this evening, Lyn."

She had forgotten. "Any excuse, Anthony Stanton, any excuse."

They both laughed, which did wonders to help Lyn let go of the anxiety she'd been experiencing for the last hour.

"Pick me up at seven, will you? The vicar will have finished evensong and be tucked up at the vicarage by then." Lyn ended the call and began to relax, and the memory of Busby faded; the soothing surroundings of farmer's fields worked their magic.

LYN'S GUESS that the reverend would be at home looked to be correct as the Morgan pulled into the sweeping drive of the sizeable Victorian building. Just one light illuminated the dark winter evening.

"You'll need to give the door knocker one heck of a bang to let him know he's got visitors."

Ant crunched his way across the gravel drive and took

heed of Lyn's advice. "Heavens, it sounds like a cavern in there."

Lyn strained to see if she could see the vicar in his drawing room. However, the net curtains were too heavily pleated for her to get a clear view. "He's bound to be at home. I've never known him to leave a light on when he leaves the place. I suppose every penny counts when you're trying to make ends meet on a modest stipend."

Ant lifted the heavy iron door knocker and brought it down with a thud on the door timbers. "He's either deaf or asleep. I'll give it one more go, then we'll have to rethink our plans for the evening."

Lyn smiled. "You mean I might get that meal after all?"

He snuck a sideways glance. "I'll be more careful about what I say in the—"

His comment was cut short by a voice from deep within the vicarage.

"Yes, yes, I'm coming."

Seconds later, a shadowy figure appeared through the mottled glass panel in the front door, which got closer and closer to the pair. After first one lock was loosened, then another, a third resulted in the door opening just wide enough for the vicar to glimpse who was calling. "Ah, it's you two. What brings you out on such a cold night?"

The door was now fully open as the clergyman stood aside to allow his visitors entry.

"Please, come through." Reverend Morton led the way into his spacious drawing room.

"Tell you what, Vicar, the Victorians certainly built big."

The vicar glanced around the cavernous space. "They specialised in big families, Anthony. I suppose the dreadful child mortality rate meant they had little choice. Unfortunately, our forebears did not envisage the high cost of electricity and gas. Now, enough of economics, to what do I owe the pleasure of your company?"

His two visitors looked at one another momentarily to see who would lead off.

"I know this may sound crackers, Reverend Morton, but we think your CCTV system might be able to tell us something about Albert Sidcup's death."

Morton shook his head. "I can't see how. As I told you both on Sunday, the signal thingy keeps breaking, so it doesn't record, or at least not for more than a second or two at a time. Blueteeth, that's what they call it, yes, I have it. The blueteeth aren't making a connection between the cameras and the computer."

The pair made a valiant effort not to laugh at the vicar's mispronunciation.

"I think you mean Bluetooth connection, Reverend," replied Lyn.

Morton still looked confused. "Do I? Oh, very well, but the outcome has been the same. The system is useless, and I found myself on lead-stealing guard again last night. It really is quite draining, you know."

The two friends nodded in sympathy of the vicar's plight.

"It must be hard for you, but surely some of your parishioners can help out?"

Morton shrugged his shoulders. "That rather depends on how you define helping out. Yes, I have had several offers but none from anyone who can move faster than a snail with its shoelaces tied together. Either that or they don't possess, or know how to work, a mobile. So even if they did see anyone, all they could do is engage them in conversation about the rights and wrongs of filching lead."

Lyn attempted to cheer the vicar up. "Never mind,

Reverend, Ant and I will help you out, won't we?" She looked across at Ant to see his eyebrows halfway up his scalp, so high were they. "You see, Ant agrees with me."

By the time the vicar glanced at Lyn's companion, he'd managed to conjure up a tortured smile hoping Morton would take the hint.

"That is so kind of you. I think the best way is for me to get a rota up so that—"

Ant had heard enough. "Er, may I suggest we look at the CCTV? Perhaps I can suggest some adjustments so that nightly vigils are only required to meet the requirements of the ecclesiastical calendar?"

Lyn choked back a giggle as she listened to Ant's pleading and watched the vicar's bemused state. "So that's it, then. Let's have a look at your troublesome technology."

Morton's confusion turned to discomfort. "But it's in the vestry; it will be freezing, and my two-bar electric fire won't touch the side of that room. We'll freeze to death. Can't this wait until the church's heating system switches on in the morning?"

Ant thought quickly to head off the vicar's reasonable request. "I do understand, Reverend. My problem is that I must deal with an important matter on behalf of my father. It is with the Lord Chamberlain, if you get my meaning. As you would expect, I can say no more than that."

Morton's eyes lit up at the mention of matters concerning the royal household. Lyn smiled at her friend's audacious fib.

"Oh, yes, I see. Of course, let us go to the vestry at once. I shall put my heavy coat on."

THE VESTRY WAS every bit as cold as the vicar had warned.

"Do forgive the electric fire. It was a gift from a long-deceased parishioner who stipulated it should reside in this room until it, too, met its demise. Unfortunately, the church is blessed with a gift that simply goes on and on despite my best attempts to sabotage the thing. Oh, does that sound uncharitable to you?"

Lyn huddled over the fire as Ant concentrated on the CCTV system.

"Can you get anything up for the night Mr Sidcup fell?"

Morton frowned as he neared a shiny black console and jabbed a finger at one of the buttons."

"I think we should start by turning the computer monitor on, don't you think, Vicar?"

Morton nodded his head. "Er, yes, that's the thing to do, isn't it?"

Ant smiled. "Yes, Vicar, I think it is. Now, let me take a look at how this thing works."

He noticed the vicar had already retreated to the electric fire.

After what seemed like an age, Ant succeeded in getting the system menu to populate the computer screen. "Now we're cooking with gas. Right, let's see what date was Tuesday. A silence made Ant turn to his two companions, who were paying not a blind bit of notice. "Thank you, yes, it was the twenty-first. Here we go, let's see what we have."

Unfortunately for Ant, there wasn't much to see. He could make out the timestamp in the bottom right-hand corner of the screen, but little else. Every so often the computer would flicker to life, but just as Ant leant into the computer to catch a detail, it returned to its blank state. "Blast this thing... oh, sorry, Vicar."

Morton stopped rubbing his hands and turned his head

towards Ant. "You are forgiven, my son. I think the Lord will recognise your valiant attempts to identify his lost sheep." With that, the reverend returned his hands to the modest heat of the electric fire.

Seconds turned to minutes as Ant tried time and time again to get some, any, image he could. Then... success.

"I've got him. I've got him." Ant was shouting and pointing at the screen.

His loud tone shook Lyn and the reverend from their slumber.

"What do you mean?" exclaimed Lyn.

"Exactly what I say. Look at the screen." Ant had paused the tape to reveal a grainy grey image of the base of the church tower and its entrance door.

"See what, exactly?" Lyn peered at the screen, getting closer and closer to see if she could identify anything. "I can't see him. You're going mad. Just because you want him to be there doesn't mean he is, Ant."

"Please, perhaps I can help." The reverend took off his glasses, then put them on again before removing them for a second time. By now his nose was almost touching the computer screen. "No, I can see nothing, if you will forgive my poor use of grammar."

Ant jabbed the screen. Lyn glared at him.

"It's no use you doing that. You can obviously see something neither the reverend nor I can. Why don't you trace an outline of what you see and give us at least a chance?"

Ant picked up on his companion's idea and extended his index finger until it touched the screen. "Now, watch." Slowly he pulled his finger over a small part of the screen and traced the outline of a figure, which almost camouflaged itself into the background.

"I see it," said the vicar.

"I don't know, oh, wait a minute," replied Lyn. "Yes, I see it."

Now that all three had managed to make out the shape, they stood back to take in the broader view.

"But how do we know it's Albert?"

Ant returned to the computer screen and pointed to two places. The first was the figure's head, the second, to a door adjacent to the form. "Do you see? Albert stood well over six feet, and I'm guessing the doorway is a standard six foot six inches tall. Now I know we have to take the camera angle into account, but I'd say for the general shape and size, together with the timestamp, it has to be our man."

The vicar nodded. "That's very clever of you, Anthony, but how does that help your investigations?"

Lyn gave her sidekick a knowing look. "I agree with the vicar."

The scepticism of his two companions amused Ant. "I don't, but it all fits. Now, if we roll the tape on and it didn't disconnect, perhaps we will see why he was there."

The two-bar electric fire was now forgotten as Ant pressed the play button and controlled the pace of film utilising a rollerball control. "There, we have him."

Again, his companions peered through half-closed eyes at the screen, attempting to view what Ant had picked up.

"Just there, can you not see? Here, let me roll the tape back a few frames then forward again. Look, he opens the door. You can just make the shadow out of the light bouncing off the strap hinges." He slowly advanced the images again. "And there, he turns around and looks at something. See the hand movement? And there, another shadow at the bottom of the screen just as the system disconnects again."

Lyn frowned. "Are you sure? Do you think that's enough to prove he was there to meet someone?"

Ant shook his head. "No, not as far as the police are concerned, but it gives us another line to follow."

The room fell silent as all three concentrated on the computer screen.

"The only thing, Anthony, is that he can't have opened that door. It's always locked except for when the bell-ringers are practising or covering a wedding and suchlike. Only I have the key."

Ant and Lyn exchanged anxious looks before he responded.

"Which can only mean two things, Vicar. Either you forgot to lock the door, or Albert, or whoever he was greeting, got access to them. Either way, we have to find out."

14

A PROPOSAL

The village coffee shop was unusually quiet for a Saturday morning.

"Where do you suppose everyone is?"

"Beats me, Lyn, but at least it'll only take Mildred a few minutes to get our full English instead of the age we normally have to wait." Ant licked his lips as he looked expectantly towards the double doors that led to the kitchen.

"You mean your full English. How you can eat all that fried food every morning is beyond me. My two rounds of toast and strawberry jam will go down very nicely with an Americano. You should try it sometimes; it might get a bit of that flab off you.

Ant feigned horror. "I'll have you know this is all muscle. Anyway, all Mildred's stuff is organic, so it must be good for keeping you fit and all that."

She shook her head. "Can I just remind you which one of us was first up those sand dunes at Horsey and which one of us almost needed oxygen?"

Ant looked sheepish, with further embarrassment saved

only by his breakfast arriving. "A load of old tosh. Now, stop being argumentative."

If his intention was to provoke her, Lyn failed to take the bait. "Speaking of arguments, I've been pondering Ron Busby again. Do you reckon someone with his temper might have actually crossed the line and got himself in real trouble?"

Ant chewed on a piece of sausage as he pondered Lyn's theory. Waving his fork like a conductor leading their orchestra, he shrugged his shoulders. "I suppose it's possible. Only one way to find out. You say he lives and works over Blickling way? Why don't you have a word with your policeman boyfriend at Cromer headquarters? They may have something on him."

Light the blue touchpaper and stand back.

"Anthony Stanton, he is not my boyfriend as you well know. I'm certain that being taken to the cinema three times when we were teenagers does not qualify for the romance-of-all-time award, stupid man." Lyn pinched the last of Ant's sausages with two fingers and fixed his gaze. He gave in first.

One of these days I'll beat you.

"Oi... cheeky madam, I was enjoying them," was the extent of the protest Ant had to offer.

"Is everything all right?" The voice from behind Ant belonged to Mildred.

He turned to face the slim woman with purple hair. "Er, oh don't mind us, we're just joking with one another."

Mildred looked confused. "I'm talking about the food, not you two daft devils. You're always the same when you're together. Always have been, always will be, that's what I say." The coffee shop owner raised her eyebrows and shook her head at both of them. "About time you two were married, that's what I say," Mildred added as she pushed her way through the kitchen swing doors.

The shop fell silent as the two friends looked nervously at one another. They tucked into the remainder of their breakfast without another word passing between them until Ant broke ranks by acting as if Mildred's aside had never happened.

"Just to let you know, I've sent the images we got from the reverend last night off to one of my mates. If anyone can clean them up, she can."

Lyn adopted a similar strategy when it came to the coffee shop owner's comment. "She?"

"Yes, Lyn. There are women in the intelligence core as well, you know. Jealous?"

"Don't you start that again, Anthony Stanton. Now, what are we going to do about Peter Lomas? Have you finalised your grand plan, then?"

Ant ignored her jibe and instead adopted a triumphant grin. "Yes, all sorted. I've had someone watch his movements, and apart from a couple of occasions where he slipped the net, I've got a fair idea what his routine is. If I'm right, he will spend most of the evening in the Rose and Crown in Saltley, pick up a pizza on the way back home, and spend the rest of the night there, and that's when we will pay him a visit. So, are you on for nine thirty tonight?"

Lyn gave him a resigned stare. "What a lovely way to spend Saturday night. Remember, I haven't forgotten about that meal you promised me."

He decided to change the subject. "And how will madam be spending the rest of the day?"

She glared at her oldest friend. "You really are pushing your luck, matey. As it happens, I plan to call in on the parents of a year-two pupil from school. One or two things I need to discuss with them, and they only live a few miles away, so it shouldn't take long."

"No rest for the wicked, is there?"

Lyn intensified her glare. "Then, in that case, you should never have a minute to yourself."

Emptying the last of their drinks, the pair made for the door at the same time as a familiar voice rang out.

"Think on you two, that's what I say."

THANK HEAVENS THAT'S DONE.

Lyn breathed a sigh of relief after spending ninety minutes with Carl Townsend's parents. It wasn't that she minded so much having to justify why their son had been put onto the class-reflective step three times in one week. What did tax her was grown-ups who believed their offspring were incapable of misbehaving.

As she walked down the long pathway from the chocolate-box cottage back to her car, Lyn rubbed her forehead to give her some relief from the headache her meeting had brought on.

Wonder if there's a chemist in the village?

As she slowly navigated her way through the twists and turns of the settlement, she almost gave up hope of medicating her sore head. Then she glanced down a small side street. Nestling between an estate agent, and newsagent cum post office, stood a tiny chemist shop. Parking her Mini, Lyn walked gingerly towards the shop, every step hurting as each foot touched the ground.

"Good afternoon, madam, how may we assist you today?"

The slim young man dressed in an immaculate white clinician's coat gave her the friendliest of greetings, which

Lyn tried hard to respond to despite her throbbing temples.

"I've a terrible headache, don't think it's migraine, but can you suggest anything for a quick fix?" Lyn rubbed the sides of her head to emphasise the point.

"I'm sure we can help, madam. Let me hand you over to my colleague, who will be pleased to make an appropriate recommendation."

It was only then that Lyn noticed the second member of staff who, until that moment, had been standing with their back towards her.

"Gosh, what a small world it is. It's Susan, isn't it? We met at the mill?"

The woman's downcast demeanour failed to lift as a flicker of recognition traced its way across the woman's face. "Oh yes, hello, you're right. My name is Susan."

At first, Lyn thought the reason for Susan's glum look was her presence triggering a memory of the previous Saturday's tragedy. She quickly reassessed when she remembered how close she seemed to have been to Albert Sidcup. "Oh, I'm sorry. Yes, of course, Albert."

Susan's dazed expression found focus on the worn lino flooring, which had, in places, worn through to reveal red tiles beneath. "He was such a nice man. I know not everyone thought so, but they didn't know him like me." Her voice trailed off.

Lyn looked at the man she had first spoken to and who appeared even more uncomfortable than she did. "It must have been such a terrible shock, Susan, and I think my presence isn't helping." Lyn looked pleadingly at the man. At last, he took the hint.

"Oh, of course, madam. Allow me to serve you. May I suggest these tablets?

Lyn took the pills without looking at them, held a debit card next to the reader and waited for five little lights on the terminal to turn green before making for the door. She glanced back to see the woman still standing motionless and looking at the floor.

———————

"So, you survived your ordeal by parents meeting, then?"

Lyn frowned at him as she checked the seal between the Morgan's soft-top and the side window. "I'm just happy that the headache has gone. It was a shocker, I tell you."

Ant watched as she traced a finger over the joint between roof and window. "What are you doing?"

She gave him a wary glance. "Remember last time you said you'd fixed the seal and I got soaked? Well, since it's throwing it down, I thought I'd play safe this time." Ignoring his indignant look, Lyn continued to check for signs of water. Satisfied that, at least on this occasion, she was likely to stay dry in the car, she relaxed back into the passenger seat. "Just an odd sort of afternoon, that's all."

He thought of probing what his friend meant before deciding to let sleeping dogs lie. Not least because of the situation they were both about to put themselves in.

As the minutes passed, the rain got heavier. The Morgan's wiper blades had difficulty dealing with the volume of water, making driving no easy task for Ant. "We'll be there in a minute, thank heavens. Are you ready for him?" Not waiting for an answer, he pulled the car to the right to avoid surface water that had gathered into a pool on a blind bend, before bringing the Morgan back over to the near side and peering out of his misted side window.

"Twenty-one, twenty-three, that's the one; look, there's a light on."

Lyn half turned to her right. "Can't see a thing. Are you sure?"

He hesitated before answering, "As sure as I can be without getting out. Now listen, let me do the talking to begin with. If he kicks off, come in with your peacemaker act, okay?"

Seconds later, they left the relative comfort of the Morgan. Now they ran as if their lives depended on it to keep as dry as possible until they reached Lomas' front door.

"At least it's got a porch," said Lyn as she huddled into Ant to avoid the worst of the weather and peered through the half-glazed door into the darkness.

Ant pressed the doorbell and waited. It seemed like an age for the hall light to illuminate the awful evening. Seconds later, the shape of someone approaching the front door gave way to it being opened, at least a little.

"Yeah?"

"Mr Lomas?" asked Ant.

"Who wants to know, then?

Ant firmed his posture, expecting trouble. He realised Lomas was having difficulty identifying the two dripping figures stood before him.

"What you want, fella?"

Lyn interjected. "We want to give you your prize, Mr Lomas. You see if we fail to deliver it, we have to go through the whole rigmarole of tracking down the next in line and possibly going through all this again. We don't get paid any extra, Mr Lomas, so please, may we come in?"

Impressive work, Lyn.

Lomas hesitated for a few more seconds before taking a step back and standing clear of the door. Ant took it not so much as a friendly invitation to enter but rather a sign he wasn't going to run for it again.

Entering the dingy living room, Ant noted the only items of any value were the oversized flat-screen TV and Apple MacBook Pro. The latter sat lazily on the stained upholstery of an old settee that sat lopsidedly opposite the TV. Just as he was about to speak, Lyn jumped in.

"I should explain about the other night. You were right; I was in the village earlier on in the day. You see, I had to check everything out with the garage owner, what's his name, er... Fitch. Well, after I'd done that, there was stuff I needed to finish back at the office in Diss. So when I said it was a bit of a run, I was truthful, but I apologise for not explaining more clearly."

Ant gave Lyn a sideways glance while maintaining a straight face.

You're becoming quite an accomplished fibber.

He could see Lyn's explanation caused Lomas to relax his posture. It now wasn't so much fight or flight as raised expectation.

"Where's my money, then?"

Lyn looked at Ant anxiously.

"What my colleague meant to say is that we now need to confirm certain details with you. After all, when dealing with such a considerable amount of cash, we need to make sure we are giving it to the correct Peter, James, Lomas. You do see, don't you?"

Ant's trap had been set. Lomas' face changed from one of avarice to utter confusion. "Wait a minute, what you talking about? I haven't got no middle name. Just Peter. What's your game?"

Ant took control, moving quickly to dominate proceedings. "Oh, dear, there seems to have been a terrible mistake.

Morticia, why have we got things mixed up? I specifically instructed you to double-check all the necessary details. As he turned from Lomas to Lyn, he winked and she would play along.

"Oh... oh, dear. I am sorry, Mr Addams. We've been so busy recently, and I, I... er, must have mixed up two files."

Ant almost let his guard down as Lyn picked up on the classic *Addams Family* TV series, which by the looks of him, aired well before Lomas was even born.

"You mean to say you have brought the twelve-month membership of the As You Like It Lady Spa Treatment Centre, instead of the two thousand pounds?"

He watched as Lomas' shoulders slumped then picked up at the mention of so much cash.

Lyn shot back in an instant. "No, no, Mr Addams. I have both prizes with me. It's just that if this gentleman does not have a middle name, then he has won the spa treatment. Is there anyone you could give the prize to, Mr Lomas?"

Lomas began to respond before choking his words off, then starting again, said, "I've just remembered. I have got a middle name, and it is Peter. It's just that we never used it at home or school, so I forgot about it."

All three looked at each other, waiting for someone to say something. Ant allowed the silence to last just long enough to catch Lomas off guard.

"Hmm, I see. Or rather, I don't... see, that is." He allowed the room to fall silent again, then struck. "I have an idea, Mr Lomas." He could feel Lyn's gaze burn into him, no doubt, he thought, to see what mess he was about to get her into. "We know certain things about the transaction at Fitch's Automotive Centre, but we haven't time to check back with the proprietor. So if you can help us, we could clear the confusion up right now, and leave having handed over your free membership, or two thousand pounds. What do you say?"

The young man began to fidget, moving from one foot to the other. Several seconds passed as his body language hardened.

"Yeh, go on, then."

Ant looked at the laptop and flat-screen TV. "Expensive, I bet?"

Lomas glanced at each. "Yeah, they was sort of payment for service rendered, if you get my meaning, and well, the rest don't matter. Now, what do you two want or I'll chuck you out now."

Lyn entered into the spirit of the evening. "What my colleague"—she looked at Ant and smiled—"Gomez, is trying to say, if I understand him correctly..." She tilted her head to one side; Ant raised an eyebrow in expectation. "Is that we know both of you had work done at the garage, but only one of you had a special feature that, how can I put this without giving you too much of a clue, makes the night into day."

Lomas looked at both of them in bemusement. "What you talking about: night, day? You talking in riddles, and I'm getting..." He paused. "Oh, I get you." Lomas broke out into a broad smile. "My racing headlamps. Bright as the sun they are. You want to see them light the road up. Dazzle anyone, they would."

"I know, Peter. They dazzled me last Saturday night."

Ant's rapid retort took Lomas by surprise. "What you mean? I weren't out last Saturday."

"I think... no. I know you were, Peter. You see, we came across each other on a quaint country road with a lovely drainage ditch to one side. Remember?"

Lomas began shuffling again. "There's no prize, is there?

What, you private detective or something, then? Well, you can sling your hook or I'll—"

"Or you'll what, Peter?" Ant pulled his frame taut; he towered over the skinny youth.

"You don't frighten me, fella. I can handle myself, I can."

Ant had a fleeting thought that youth combined with a taste for self-survival might trump his military experience. The moment of doubt passed quickly. "I'm sure you can. The question is, do you want to take the risk?"

Lomas walked over to the half-closed lounge door and pulled it wide open. "Out you go, or I'm calling the police."

Lyn couldn't help letting out a throaty laugh, which appeared to distract Lomas.

Ant reached for his mobile. "Do you want to borrow mine, or should I ring Detective Inspector Riley?"

The youth froze at the mention of the policeman's name. "Do what you want, pal, but her and you are leaving now. I've got mates, you know."

Ant smiled, which had the desired effect of making Lomas even jumpier. "I'm sure you have, what, like the ones that gave you the laptop and telly?"

It was Lomas' turn to smile now. "You ain't got a clue, have you? Now clear off."

Ant had one more trick up his sleeve. "Then we'll just have to inform the authorities about your car."

The young man froze. "What you mean?"

He let the youth stew for a few seconds without taking his eyes off him. "You see, Peter, we've been doing some checks on you, just as my friend, Morticia, said. What we didn't tell you is what those checks covered. I should tell you we do a very thorough job, and it seems you neither have car insurance nor tax for your car, do you? Oh, and for a full house, you haven't bothered to MoT the vehicle for the last two years."

Lomas looked stunned. "Yes I have; you can check the records."

"As I said, Peter, we have checked the records. There are documents on file for your make and colour of car. It's just that they don't refer to your car, do they?"

The youth drained of colour and quietly closed the hall door. Leaning against the peeling paintwork of the architrave, Lomas looked forlornly at Ant. "What do you want from me?"

"That's better, Peter. Now come and sit on your lovely sofa, and tell me all about Saturday night and Bampton Mill."

Lomas paced over to the threadbare seat and slumped into its worn-out cushions. "Bampton Mill, what you talking about, man?"

Ant looked across to Lyn then back to Lomas. "Now, Peter, let's not start that nonsense again. You were at Bampton Mill on Saturday night and ran me off the road. Is that not correct?"

He stood over the slouching youth, making the differences in the height all the more noticeable. Dominating the space was something he had been trained to do. He used it to good effect.

"Do we inform the authorities, or does this stupidity stop now?"

Lomas looked at the laptop, then the vast TV screen before looking in Ant's direction, but without making eye contact.

"It was me at Bampton Mill."

15

IT WAS ME

Peter Lomas sat quietly on the sofa after blurting out his stark admission.

Flanked on each side by Ant and Lyn, the young man stared at the blank TV screen.

"Okay, Peter, now we're getting somewhere. What we need you to tell us now is why you were at the mill." Ant's voice was calm, controlled, and assertive. The clipped tone he rarely gave away in normal conversation was now present. Received English, as adopted by the social elite in Victorian times had its uses. Typically considered pompous, it could be put to productive use in the circumstances in which the two friends now found themselves.

Lomas glared at Ant. "I told you I was there. You don't need to know why. That's all I'm saying." The young man folded his arms across his chest and resumed watching a blank screen.

Ant gave Lyn the slightest of nods to indicate it was time for the good cop.

"Listen, Peter. We know tonight has been a terrible shock for you, and we certainly do not want to get you getting into trouble with the police. The problem is, though, a terrible thing happened at that mill last Saturday. It's something the police will not let go of, and if we managed to track you down, the police aren't going to be far behind, are they?"

His closing question caused Lomas to sit bolt upright and vary his glare between his two interrogators. "What you talking about, woman?"

Ant shot Lyn a look to see if Lomas' discourtesy would rattle Lyn. It was clear it hadn't.

"You mean, you don't know?" She intentionally gave her last word an upward inflexion.

"Know what? You gone mad, you have, woman."

Ant took over. "Mr Lomas, Burt Bampton died at that mill last Saturday. The police think it's murder, so what do you think they've been doing all week? Eating chocolate doughnuts and binging on a box set of *Dixon of Dock Green*?"

Lomas sprang to his feet. Ant braced himself for violence.

"I don't know nothing about that fella dying. Nothing to do with me, mate. I ain't saying nothing more. If the cops come, I'll tell them you was trying to fit me up. Now get out."

―――――

THERE WERE FEWER BETTER treats than sitting below deck on his father's wherry, *Field Surfer*, on a cold winter's day snuggled by the stove. At least that was Ant's assessment as he and Lyn discussed the events of the previous evening over a steaming mug of freshly ground coffee.

"Well, he certainly has a temper, that's for sure. Perhaps he and Burt had fallen out over something and found a way to kill him?"

Ant warmed both hands on his mug of coffee as he

listened to her theory. "I'm not sure. I think his skull is too thick for much other than superficial stuff to get him going. Think of how he behaved last night. Say one thing to him, and he's all smiles; change tack, and he's at your throat. If Burt was murdered, whoever planned and carried it through was much more sophisticated than Lynx man; did you catch a whiff of him?"

Lyn nodded. "Was a bit overpowering, wasn't it? You know, if I think about it, his appearance was the opposite of the state of his house. The place reeked while he looked as though he'd just been kitted out at Ralph Lauren. Where does the money come from to look like that?"

"Beats me, unless, of course, he's stealing stuff and selling it on for cash?"

Allowing their ideas to consolidate for a few seconds, both took a long, slow sip of coffee.

"Won't be long before you'll be moving *Field Surfer* from her winter moorings and getting things ready for Easter?" Lyn's change of direction acted as light relief for Ant. "You're right. Another couple of weeks, and it'll be time to give the girl a good spring clean. Are you up for it?"

Lyn smiled. "You ask me that every year when you're at home. I might have asked you that question, since when you were away, I de-winterised her."

He returned her smile. In an instant, he morphed from a relaxed posture to highly animated. "Wait a minute, you may have a point."

"What, about me doing stuff when you're away playing soldiers?"

Ant waved his hands as if cleaning an imaginary white-board. "No, no, not that; you said, getting things ready. Perhaps that's what Lomas did, then had to go back to retrieve the evidence from the mill before the police found it." He stood up and stepped the few feet required to look out of the cabin window. In the distance he could just make out Bampton Mill on top of one of the few rises in landscape for miles around. "What if last Saturday night was all about retrieval rather than stealing, and when he heard the Morgan, he knew he had to get out of there pretty sharpish?"

Lyn joined him. "You're not making sense, Ant. You said yourself that when you and Fitch went into the mill, nothing looked out of place." She paused then pointed a finger. "Looking at Bampton Mill now, you wouldn't think it's been a place of such misery, would you?"

He didn't respond. Instead, he made for his drink and drained the last of the coffee. "I dunno, Lyn, but the longer this goes on, the less chance we will have of finding the truth behind our friend's death. Come on, I'll drop you off at home."

Lyn shrugged her shoulders before following him up on deck.

———

"WELL, it makes a nice change to finish a journey in this old thing, and I'm still dry and don't need to go back to the hairdressers." Lyn gave Ant a lofty look as she opened the Morgan's passenger door and clambered out.

"Don't slam the d— " It was too late. Lyn shut the door with such force that the windscreen wipers momentarily lifted from the glass. "You always do that."

Lyn looked at him dismissively. "And I've told you a hundred times to get that silly catch fixed. If you think I'm going to muck about every time I get out, you can think again, sunshine. Now, do you want Sunday lunch or not?"

Ant weighed up his options. To protest might mean

going without Lyn's stupendous Yorkshire puddings. He
decided on a token rebuke. "You do talk rubbish sometimes."
He watched her bristle. "But on this occasion, I am prepared
to concede you have a point."

She gave him a wry smile. "You mean you want lunch,
Anthony Stanton."

An hour later, and they were back on Lyn's doorstep
making their farewells.

"It's agreed, then. You'll nip back to Burt's wife to see if
there's anything else she can tell us, and I'll check to see if
I've had any results on the things I kicked off since last
Saturday."

She nodded then let out a sigh.

"Something up, Lyn?"

His friend looked towards her car. "I forgot; I need to get
rid of that rubbish I stupidly agreed to dump with the river
warden. The problem is the recycling centre will be closed
now, and it won't all fit in my bin."

Ant walked the few feet to Lyn's car. "Give it here. I'll get
rid of it in one of the estate skips."

Disappearing for a few seconds, Lyn re-emerged from
the hallway, car keys in hand. "You see, you do have your
uses after all." Her smile broadened as she raised the boot
and peered into the small space. "For the love of... look, the
bag's come undone. There's stuff all over the place."

Ant began laughing as he caught sight of the mess. Have
you another sack? I'll start to gath—" He broke off mid-
sentence as his eyes darted from one object to another
among the scene of chaos. "Something's changed. That's
what I said ages ago. Something has changed, haha." Ant
clapped his hands so loud that it startled Lyn and caused
Phyllis and Betty, who were passing on the opposite side of
the narrow road, to tut tut in a loud tone.

"This is getting to be a habit, Ant. What on earth is going on this time?" She looked back into her boot.

"Don't you see? They've changed."

Lyn glared at him. "If you say that one more time, I'll tip the lot over you, do you hear? Now talk in plain English."

Ant took a step back so that Lyn could get a more detailed view. "Tell me what you see?"

She moved forward a few feet and examined the rubbish strewn about on the boot lining. "Papers, sweet wrappings, er, a newspaper, and a load of paper cups."

"Spot on," exclaimed Ant, almost unable to contain his excitement.

She looked over her shoulder at Ant. "I'm warning you."

He let out a throaty laugh. "The paper cups, don't you get it?"

Lyn let out a shriek of frustration.

"If I have this right, it will all become clear by the end of the day. But first, we both need to check a couple of things out. By the way, have you still got those pictures you took at the mill?"

Lyn nodded, still looking bemused.

"Good, what I need you to do is..."

———

"HELLO. You took some finding; I've almost worn out a pair of trainers from walking so far."

The river warden gave a chortle as he greeted Lyn. "Ah, well, I told you I come a lot farther up the broad during the winter." He offered Lyn a seat next to him, which overlooked a long stretch of Hickham Broad.

"Thanks, Stan. I know, but there's walking, then there's hiking. I'll say this, the area you cover must keep you fit. Do the authorities pay for your footwear? If they don't, I imagine you must really be out of pocket."

Stan laughed as he reached for a paper bag in one of several pockets in his winter jacket. "Want one?"

Lyn peered into the half-open bag. "Hmm, I haven't seen rhubarb-and-custard-boiled sweeties for years. Where on earth do you get them?"

The river warden took his turn in rummaging through the bag before popping one in his mouth. "On the internet, like most things these days. And tell you what, they're not thruppence for two ounces anymore either. Those were the days, eh?"

She almost choked on the confectionary at the mention of predecimal money. "I'm not that old, Stan. Thanks a bunch."

"Oops, sorry. Of course, you're not. Still nice, though, aren't they, eh?"

She gave his shoulder a friendly bump as they spent a couple of minutes enjoying the tranquil scene of still water. An occasional heron flew overhead while brief bursts of relative warmth bathed them as the winter sun shone through high banks of translucent clouds.

"You've still not told me why you've trekked all the way up here to see me, Lyn?" Stan offered Lyn a second sweet before returning the bag to his pocket.

She held a finger of recognition up as she pulled her mobile from a pocket with her free hand. "Ah, I almost forgot. Right, I wonder if you can help me with something?" Lyn tapped a code into the phone and flicked through several images until she found the one she'd been looking for. "Do you recognise anyone in this photograph?"

Stan took the mobile and turned it through ninety

degrees to get a better look at the image. After a few seconds, he pointed at part of the picture. "That one."

Lyn looked closely to where the river warden was pointing. She looked confused. "Are you sure, Stan? Take another look."

Stan brushed the phone away. "It's that one all right, like I said the other day, Lyn. I never forget a face."

"MUM'S just gone for a walk, but she won't be much longer. I think she needed some time on her own." The voice of Sophie, Jennifer's daughter, was strong and understanding. Lyn marvelled at the maturity of the teenager coming to terms with the death of her father yet thinking of her mother's need for space.

"Oh, that's okay. I can call back later." Lyn made to turn and walk back to her car when the girl intervened.

"Don't be daft; you've come all this way, and as I said, Mum will be here soon. Why don't you come in?"

Lyn hesitated for a second not wanting to bother the girl at such a difficult time. The need to find answers led her to put the feelings aside. "Well, if you don't mind. I'll give it ten minutes then get out of your hair."

Sophie was already pointing towards the kitchen.

"Can I help at all?"

The girl's directness took Lyn by surprise.

I wonder?

"Well, I don't want to bother you, but I just wanted to ask your mum. You see, she's mentioned a couple of times recently that people sometimes asked your dad if he wanted to sell the mill. Now I know he would never have done that, but I just need to check it out."

Sophie shrugged her shoulders. "All the time. Some were nice, others a bit rude. A couple even tried to get me to talk to Dad, would you believe that?"

Lyn's curiosity grew. "You? How awful. It never ceases to surprise me how far people will go when they really want something."

The teenager nodded. "You're telling me. A couple of them especially. Always on the phone and stuff like that, even came around the other day to give Mum a card for Dad, but I knew what they wanted. I never told Mum, but when she went to make them a cup of tea, I came across them rummaging through some of Dad's drawers. They didn't see me, and I've not said anything, but if they come back, I'll give them what for."

Lyn could hardly keep a lid on her excitement. "So you would recognise them if you saw them again?"

"From a mile away, no problem."

Time to go for it.

Lyn, once more, took out her mobile and showed the same image that she'd asked the river warden to look at.

"That one."

The teenager's lack of hesitation startled Lyn.

The same person; what's going on?

Lyn knew she needed to get back to tell Ant. Was she to wait for Sophie's mother to return or leave now? Her investigation won the argument.

"Sophie, I need to go now, but please be sure to tell your mum I popped over, and what we've talked about today. Do you understand? Tell her I will be in touch this evening and that I must talk to her."

The teenager nodded, giving Lyn a look that led her to think the girl couldn't see what all the fuss was about. That was a position she was content with.

"You took your time. Was traffic bad or something?"

"I'll give you bad traffic. We don't all drive like Lewis Hamilton, you know." Lyn ignored Ant's welcoming smile as she stepped to his side and entered the already open door of Bampton Mill. "And before we start, I'm in no mood for more of your 'guess what's changed' game. I've told you what Stan and Jennifer's daughter have confirmed, so why don't we go to the police right now?"

Her challenge wasn't what he'd been expecting.

Should have worked out what this stuff takes out of her.

Ant followed and quietly shut the heavy wooden door behind them. The interior delivered the solitude and quietness he'd experienced the week before, giving away not the slightest hint of the tragedy it hid within its ancient walls.

"Fair enough, Lyn; no more games, then. Except I just want you to look at the tabletop. Remember, that's where Burt set out the paper cups ready for the Windy Wanderers."

Stepping confidently across to the table, the only thing disturbing the absolute quiet was an occasional creak coming from the machine gearing as the mill sails attempted to untether themselves.

"I see, well, actually, I don't see anything?"

Ant joined her. "Take a step back and look again. What is it that isn't there?" He caught a glimmer of her nostrils starting to flare. "Okay, okay." He held his arms up to recognise Lyn's dominance on the matter. "I only see six cups, and all of them are huddled towards the centre of the table." He looked at Lyn for any sign of recognition. There was none. "Well, there were three of us and twelve of them, and I know that Burt put some extra out. Well, where have they all gone?"

It was then Lyn caught on and immediately glanced beneath the table. Her positive expression faded."

Ant moved forward until his legs touched the side of the tabletop. "I bet your schoolkids love doing this." He extended a forefinger and traced a smiley face shape by cutting through the fine layer of grain dust that covered everything in the mill. Lyn's eyes lit up.

"Look, you can tell that something has sort of swept the right half of the surface."

He clapped his hands together, this time more quietly so as not to make her jump. "Someone, not something, Lyn. Whoever did that wanted it badly, and they were working fast. The question is, where did they put whatever it was in?"

Lyn looked under the table again. "Ah, I see."

He joined her. "Get it? It's about what's not there rather than what we can see."

Lyn traced a finger on the stone floor that followed the outline of where a circular object had stopped dust from gathering. "I remember now; there was a wastepaper basket here. Look, you can see the shape of its base."

Ant stood upright and waited for Lyn to do the same. "Got it in one, Lyn." She looked back at the dust shadow then to her companion. "So you're saying Lomas did break in last Saturday and stole a load of paper cups by sweeping them into a wastepaper bin? Do you think they knew each other?"

Ant completed a final visual sweep of the ground floor before answering.

"It's perfectly possible, Lyn. We now just need to prove how."

16

A MESSY UNDOING

Breakfast at Stanton Hall followed its usual routine: the Earl of Stanton seated by eight and his son sauntering in forty-five minutes later, meaning he often ate alone. Today was different.

"Thank you for joining me, son."

The earl's voice was a little too thin for Ant's liking.

"Is anything wrong, Dad? I thought the hospital said they expected to discharge Mum today?" They both looked at an empty dining chair.

"Well, that was the plan, Anthony, but I'm afraid to say they have found something they are not at all happy with..." The earl's voice trailed off.

This is not like Dad.

Ant bit half-heartedly at a piece of dry brown toast. "Come on, Dad. You always say we can deal with what we know rather than fret about unknowns."

His father offered a half-smile. "You're right, of course. It's just that the news has come as a bit of a shock. Nevertheless, as you say, we must get on with things. I received a call overnight from the surgeon informing me your mother was in the operating theatre. It seems her condition suddenly took a turn for the worse. I don't know all the details, but they had to move quickly. In itself, the doctors tell me it's a routine procedure, but what with her other ailments and age, they say there is a much higher risk all may not go to plan. Do you understand, son?"

Ant distracted himself by putting too much sugar into his coffee, tasting it and scrunching his face up. The adult had turned back into a child, relying on its father for comfort. "When do you expect to hear something? Shouldn't we be at the hospital?"

His father shook his head. "No, they specifically said they would ring as soon as they were 'closing up' as the surgeon put it, so if we went now, we'd be sat looking at those awful cream walls in the waiting room."

That's the spirit, Dad.

"So, we just wait?"

"We just wait, son."

Minutes passed like hours, then the phone rang.

Ant sprang to his feet and shot over to the old-fashioned telephone, which rested on an eighteenth-century half-round games table.

"Yes, I'm Lady Stanton's son... yes, my father is with me... I see... and the implications?... I understand. Yes, thank you for informing me. I shall inform the earl immediately... and thank you so much for all you have done. We all owe you so much."

Ant slowly placed the handset into its cradle, turned to his father without showing any reaction, and quietly walked back to the breakfast table. He selected a second slice of bread from the toast rack, this time remembering to butter it.

"I see," murmured the earl. Well, there will be a lot to

organise. Can you call the clan together, son? I shall inform her closest friends."

Ant had held it together just long enough to finish his toast. "I think you are a little premature, Father. When Mr Prentice left Mum, she was already coming around and demanding a cup of tea and her favourite garibaldi biscuits."

The earl's face lit up before he quickly regained control. "Anthony, you will be the death of me one day. Now, pass me the marmalade. I have a busy day ahead since it seems your mother will command my presence soon. And you, what are you up to?"

Ant was having trouble eating and laughing at the same time. He knew his father had the temperament of steel so could put up with his japes. "I'll want to call in on Mum later, of course, but first I have to catch up with Lyn, then get things ready at Bampton Mill."

His father frowned. "Bampton Mill, what are you—oh, I see. You're going to do one of your Hercule Poirot whodunnits, are you?"

Ant laughed as he reached for a sausage, bit it in half, and wagged the remainder at the earl. "Quite so, Father, quite so."

———

"THAT WAS A CLOSE CALL, THEN?" Lyn took hold of Ant's hand as they sat at her kitchen table, sharing a packet of Maltesers.

"You know Mum, always does the unexpected. Still, she'll have to take it easy when they get her home."

"Good luck with that," replied Lyn as her smile broadened into an all-out giggle.

A few seconds of quiet followed as both looked at their intertwined hands.

"Anyway, back to business, Lyn." He slipped his fingers from Lyn's and started fidgeting. "Lots to do today. Virtually everything is in place. I just need to ready the mill for our little get-together as long as you can make sure everyone arrives on time. Don't take any excuses. If you tell them what I said, they'll turn up, I promise you."

She looked at him. "Virtually? I thought you said it all fitted together nicely?"

"And so it does, or rather it will be once Fitch joins the party to confirm one or two things."

Lyn shook her head. "So when you say we are ready to solve the case, you actually mean we might be about to solve it. Except we will have half a dozen possible suspects in front of us. Oh, and not forgetting your favourite detective?"

"That about sums it up, Lyn. What's to worry about?"

BAMPTON MILL WAS at its most atmospheric when backlit by a bright full moon. Ant took a minute to walk a hundred yards west of the ancient construction to take in the eerie sight of the mill. Its crown was bathed in the soft moonlight and the sails standing sentry over a deserted landscape.

As he flicked the lock open and stepped inside the familiar surroundings, he stood for a moment in awe of the beam of light that had penetrated the first-floor window. It cast a soft, luminescent hue throughout the ground floor.

I wonder?

Ant played with lighting levels caused by trying multiple combinations to give him the atmosphere he intended for the evening's main event. Allowing the external light to take precedence, he complemented the effect with two desk lamps. His assumption was Burt must have used them when the mill wasn't in full swing.

That's got it, Burt, we'll both do you proud, I promise you.

Ant felt a pang of disappointment that the arrival of first one car, then another, interrupted the moment with his old friend. Then the adrenalin kicked in. He was ready.

"All okay?" Lyn spoke softly in the serene surroundings Ant had created. "They're all coming, even Riley, but he's not happy."

"When was the man ever happy?" Ant smiled and told Lyn where he wanted her to stand. "At the bottom of the steps, please. They'll wonder what I'm up to, but that's no bad thing."

Seconds later, the sound of a dog barking and its owner trying unsuccessfully to control the animal pierced the quiet.

"If you don't stop that, Daddy will be cross, and there'll be no biscuits for you, my lad."

Curious, Ant popped his head around the open mill door to see Riley struggling to tether his dog to a hitching post meant for horses. "Ah, Detective Inspector, or should I call you Daddy? Very pleased you could come."

Riley scowled first at his dog, who continued to misbehave until its owner dropped two doggie treats at its feet, then at Ant.

"I hope you know I'm on leave this week and do not take kindly to being dragged out here on a wild-goose chase. If you've dragged me away from Aretha Franklin for nothing, I shall take the greatest pleasure in finally arresting you and Girl Friday for wasting police time. Do you understand me?"

Ant gave the detective an earnest look before glancing down at the dog. "I always say the answer lies in bribery, wouldn't you agree, Detective Inspector?" He didn't wait for the incandescent detective to respond. "Now, do come in. We are expecting the others in a few minutes."

"Detective Inspector Riley, so nice to see you." Lyn's friendly greeting served only to increase Riley's ire.

"Listen, I'm here, aren't I, so let's get it over and done with, but as I warned Batman, there, if you are wasting my time, I'll—"

Riley's words were cut short by Peter Lomas entering the mill. His face turned ashen as he saw the policeman.

"Well, who do we have here? If it isn't Lowlife Lomas. Nobody told me you were out, and I'm sure it won't be long before you attract our attention again. You never know, tonight may be the night, so to speak."

Peter Lomas tried to ignore the detective as Ant pointed to one of the chairs that made up a half crescent.

Next to arrive was Ron Busby. As he crossed the threshold, he swept a hand across his comb-over. He looked first at Lyn, then Ant, then finally the detective.

"Well, well, you don't see a criminal for ages, then two come along within seconds. How's life treating you now you're out of prison... again?"

Ant noted Riley's mood was improving by the minute. "Do come and join us, Ron. This won't take long."

Busby avoided further eye contact with the policeman and placed himself on a chair as far away from Lomas as was possible.

Following the rattle of a bicycle falling against the mill, in walked the vicar.

"I don't believe it" Riley chortled. "This is better than a game of Clue. We only need the butler, a lead pipe, a candlestick, and we've got the lot. You two really are a joke, and you've got fifteen minutes before I take my dog home, while you spend a night in the cells." Riley fixed his gaze on Lyn before redirecting his attention to Ant.

Neither responded to the detective's bait.

The vicar muttering under his breath as he fought to remove his bicycle clips, broke the tension.

"Can I help?"

"Quite all right. I think I've—" Reverend Morton's confidence was misplaced as one of the clips shot from his ankle, bounced off a roof beam, and kissed Riley's cheek on its way to the floor.

"That's it. That's enough of this nonsense. I'm off. You two will be spending tonight at the police station. As for the rest of you—get lost."

Ant's plan was only saved by the diminutive figure of Susan Mylnweard stepping quietly into the mill.

"I had a message to pop over here; is everything all right?" She concentrated on the vicar as the man scrambled to retrieve his errant bicycle clip.

"Yes, yes, everything is just fine." Ant tried to sound as calm as possible. "Do come and join us, and I'll explain why Lyn and I have dragged you all out on a cold Monday evening."

He glanced nervously at Riley and was relieved to see he had settled back into his chair.

"Ladies and gentlemen, I think we are just about ready to start." Ant positioned himself with his back to the potbelly stove he'd almost been impaled by on the previous Saturday and surveyed the faces before him. Except for Riley's usual sour expression, he noted the others wore a combination of nervousness and curiosity. No one looked more unsettled than his or her neighbour.

Have I got this wrong?

Ant hesitated for a few seconds as he mentally ran

through what he was about to say. "Last Saturday a tragedy happened in this place." Ant looked at where Lyn was standing. Everyone else turned to glance at the steep steps. "The police think Burt Bampton's death was an accident, pure and simple, and I understand why."

Riley's head popped up at the mention of the force. "Because it was an accident, and that's all there is to it. Now, where is your nonsense taking us?"

Ant smiled. "All in good time, Detective Inspector."

Riley shook his head and resumed looking at the stone floor.

"The Windy Wanderers were welcomed by Burt as a group of friendly people of a certain age with a common interest, and I thank two of their group for being here this evening."

Ron and Susan acknowledged his citation with a small nod. "It was a sombre day, Lord Stanton, and not one I, or my fellow members, will forget lightly." Susan's eyes filled with tears as she spoke.

Riley sighed and looked at his watch.

"Thank you, Susan. It was a great shock to us all. Of course, like all groups, the Wanderers have their characters. Some members are inevitably more popular than others. Dare I say some members are actively disliked by others, isn't that right, Ron?"

Busby's eyes bulged at being singled out. He swept a hand across his comb-over and started to cross, then uncross his legs. "Why do you say that to me? I get on with most people most of the time. Are you asking me a question or just making an observation?" He glared at Ant, who could see he was having difficulty keeping his temper in check.

"You see, that's the problem. Just as you are getting defensive and angry now, so you did when Burt made an ill-judged joke about your hair failing to protect your head on the low headroom when getting to the second floor."

Again, heads turned as this time they looked up in the direction of the first-floor bulkhead through which the old steps passed.

"I didn't say anything to Mr Bampton?"

"You didn't need to. I could see your reaction as I'm sure the others did."

Susan stretched out a sympathetic hand to her fellow group member. "It's okay, Ron, don't worry about it."

"But that wasn't all, was it, Ron? A few minutes later, I had to pull poor Burt off the railings up there." Ant pointed to an upper floor, all eyes followed his finger. "Was it just a coincidence you were there as well, or did you try to push him? Certainly, Burt thought so."

The detective inspector came to life once more. "No one told me about this?" His intense tone chilled the atmosphere.

"I told you at the time, I tripped and fell into him. Simple as that. You saw how rotten that rail was. How could I have known that—I'd never been here before last weekend?"

Unseen by all except Ant and Lyn, the mill door had been opened, and a woman stood, her frame backlit by the clear night sky.

"That's not true, is it, Mr Busby? You came weeks before to ask my husband if your group could visit the mill. He told me you sounded angry when he refused and thought you were going to hit him. It was only when the other one arrived you calmed down, and my husband agreed to the visit."

Riley's gaze burned into Burt's widow, Jennifer. "Are you telling me there had already been an altercation between your husband and this man?"

Jennifer stepped through the doorway; her tear-stained face open for all to see. "I'm not saying they argued; I wasn't here. All I can tell you is my husband was left unsettled."

Ant pressed on without giving Busby a chance to respond to the widow. Lyn put her arm around Jennifer and guided her to a seat next to her by the stairway.

"And then we have Mr Lomas. Now, Peter is a bit of a mystery man, or at least that's the image he likes to portray, isn't that right, Peter?"

Lomas shrugged his shoulders as he slumped in the chair, his legs fully extended and crossed at the ankle.

"You see, this young man likes his fast cars. He also likes the latest technology—computers, TVs, that sort of thing. The only problem is, he can't afford such things. Isn't that right, Peter?"

Riley answered for the young man, "Been stealing and fencing swag all his life, that one. Looks like you've been up to your old tricks. I told you half an hour ago our paths would cross before long. Even I didn't think it would be this quick." For the first time that evening, the detective smiled. "Is that it, then? Are you saying these two arranged Mr Bampton's accident to clean him out? If you are, then give me the evidence so I can get back to listening to my Aretha Franklin collection."

Both Busby and Lomas shot to their feet. Ant held out a calming hand as Riley started to move forward.

"Not so hasty, my friends. Let's all sit down and relax because I have more to tell you."

Lyn gave Jennifer a reassuring rub on her arm, stood up, and quietly moved around to one side of the doorway.

"You can see my problem, can't you, Peter, Mr Busby? We have an older man who is vain, has a short temper, and has previous convictions for grievous bodily harm. And we have a younger man who wants to own the best things but cannot afford them without resorting to the sort of thing the good Detective Inspector Riley takes a keen interest in. Am I correct?"

The two men shifted uncomfortably in their chairs without exchanging glances. It was Busby who shouted first.

"I do not know this man, I have never met him, and from what you say, have not the slightest thing in common with him."

"I know," said Ant quietly. It didn't stop Lomas jumping to his feet.

"And I've never seen that old bloke before, and he didn't pay for my car or the other stuff, see?"

"I agree," commented Ant for the second time.

The room fell into silence as Ant's responses finally sank in.

Riley sighed. "Then for the love of wet fish and my sanity, what *are* you saying?"

Ant smiled and looked across at Lyn, who had opened the door and had her head outside the mill. "I'm saying that as well as liking the good things in life, young Peter here is a bit of a lady's man. Isn't that right, Peter?"

Lomas stared at Ant, the aggression had gone, now replaced by a look of fear.

"You see, when this young man ran us off the road last Saturday evening, it wasn't because he was responsible for the break-in. What neither my friend Fitch nor I considered was that there were two people in the car as it hurtled towards us. After all, the headlights were so bright we couldn't see a thing. And if Peter hadn't made the mistake of getting his exhaust fixed locally at Fitch's place, we'd have been none the wiser. Bad luck, eh, Peter?"

The detective inspector got to his feet once again. "For

the last time, Little Lord Fauntleroy, where are you going with this tripe?"

His nemesis smiled. "Not long now, Inspector."

Riley paced the small space behind the crescent of chairs before lounging against an old store cupboard. Meanwhile, Lomas became more and more agitated.

"You talking rubbish, mate. Honest, you is."

Ant shot back at the youth, "Does the name Patricia Melling mean anything to you, Peter?"

It was if a bolt of lightning had struck Lomas. "Pat... er, no. Don't know what you mean. Melling? Who are they when they're at home?"

His interrogator closed the distance between them. "In a nutshell, that's your problem, isn't it, Peter? You see, I don't mean just any Melling. I'm referring to the Mrs Melling who is married to Alfred Melling, the owner of the largest car dealership for miles around. I'm told he is a jealous man with some fascinating friends who will do anything he asks."

Lomas looked towards the door, then at Ant, whose eyes were firmly fixed on the youth's chair. He took the hint.

Riley let out a throaty laugh. "Well, well, who's been a naughty boy, then? If Tiny Melling gets his hands on you, you'll need more than a fast car to get out of his way."

Ant moved towards Lomas, thinking he was about to pass out. "Sit down, Peter. That's the worst over."

The young man looked expectantly up at Ant.

"Now, while I can't get you out of trouble with her husband, if indeed he's aware of your, shall we say, interest, I can give you some advice." He smiled at Lomas. "Stick to girls that are single and unattached, and don't think you can keep any secrets in a place as small as Stanton Parva. You were seen by someone who knew you and your preference for wealthy married women who like to buy you presents, when you brought your car in for repair. Don't ask me who it was because it doesn't matter. Suffice it to say, once we traced you, it wasn't hard to find out what you got up to. Oh, and that's another thing. Do vary your routine, Peter. It took Lyn and me three days to catch on. How long do you think it will take Tiny Melling and his mates?"

"Time for a holiday a long way away, I think, Lomas. I can fix it in one of Her Majesty's big hotels if you want?"

Ant didn't take kindly to the detective's repeated hints at prison as the solution to all things. "Think on, Peter. I've heard Devon is nice this time of year, and the caravan sites will be open soon."

The young man's shoulders had visibly relaxed as he listened to Ant's advice. However, it didn't go unnoticed that he was smiling at Susan, who seemed to be returning the compliment.

"Take note of what I said, Peter," barked Ant.

In all the confusion, he noticed Busby had started to enjoy himself. It was time to change that state of affairs.

"So, what about you, Ron? Where does that leave things?"

Busby's grin vanished in a second. "What do you mean?"

"Well, we have a man that died on a step where you and him had argued and were immediately above when he fell, you know, your feet within inches of Burt's head and shoulders. It would have been easy enough for you to have given him a nudge. Then we have the break-in. Perhaps it was you who picked the lock to retrieve something from earlier that day, which might have implicated you in Burt's death. What do you say, Ron?"

Riley roused himself from his slouching position against the cupboard. "So, you think he's our man, supposing Mr

Bampton was killed. I do suppose you have concrete evidence rather than this homespun nonsense."

Ant looked towards the door and saw Fitch being quietly welcomed by Lyn. He waited for a split second while he caught his friend's eye. Fitch nodded.

"You're right," replied Ant quietly.

Riley turned purple with rage while Busby leant back in his chair."

"Then what the blazes are you—"

"You see, Mr Busby didn't kill Burt Bampton." He hesitated before turning slightly. "It was you, wasn't it, Susan?"

The room erupted as Riley began screaming at Ant for wasting his time. Busby looked at the woman in horror, and Lomas began to laugh.

"Enough!" shouted Lyn, who still stood at the open door. "Listen to the rest of it." She glared at the detective.

Riley fell quiet. Susan sat immobile, her face motionless. She began to speak so quietly that it was difficult for the others to make out.

"How can you think that? He was such a kind man. I liked him a lot."

Ant knelt down in front of Susan, his face contorted with sadness. "That's the problem, isn't it, Susan? Those you get close to, or you think like you, tend to get hurt, don't they?"

Susan looked at Ant, her eyes streaming with tears. Ron Busby went to hold her hand; she snatched it away. "Do we have to do this? Haven't you done enough damage tonight, Ant, er Anth—or whatever we're supposed to call you?"

"Hear, hear," snarled the detective as he made for the door.

"Mylnweard is a strange surname, isn't it, Susan?"

The woman stared at Ant without saying a word.

"It turns out your family has lived in Norfolk for generations. I'm ashamed to say you lot have been here longer than my own family, so Lyn and I were intrigued enough about your name to do a bit of digging. I'm sure everyone here will be interested to know that Mylnweard is Anglo Saxon for mill keeper, or 'to grind.' Did you know that, Susan?" His question was met with no reply. "Of course, you did, and that's at the heart of this mystery. You see, we know you wanted to buy a mill. Not any old mill though. You believed Burt's ancestors cheated you out of this mill, and you wanted it back, and when Burt wouldn't sell it to you, you decided he had to go."

Ant now had Riley's full attention. "I assume you can prove this."

He looked at the detective with conviction in his eyes. "Oh yes, Detective Inspector Riley, I can prove it."

Susan looked across towards the open doorway.

"Too late for that, Susan. And you know what, if you had played things differently, you might have got away with it. You played a perfect hand in calming Albert Sidcup down when he continuously heckled Burt about how much the mill was worth. That was very clever and kept you off Lyn's and my radar for quite a time. But then you made a stupid mistake. You were seen walking away from the mill, isn't that correct, Peter?"

The young man was startled, thinking he was under suspicion again.

"It's okay, Peter, I just want you to confirm you saw someone running down to the broad?"

Lomas nodded. "But I told you I didn't see who it was."

Susan appeared to relax.

"No, no, Susan, you're not off the hook yet. You see, although we can't prove you broke in or dropped the lock key we found, I—"

Riley flew into another temper. "Break-in, lock picks. Who do you think you are to keep evidence from the police?"

"Don't take that tone with me, man. You are the one who, as usual, wanted to close the case prematurely. You were the one that insisted one of my best friends simply fell off a set of steps he'd used for decades without incident. You are the one that appears more interested in getting back to his record collection than listening to what actually happened. Now, if you want to stop this now and arrest Lyn and me, go ahead. I'm sure the chief constable will be delighted you let another case slip through your fingers. Now, what do you want to do? Arrest a killer or fill your cells with people who are trying to help? You decide, Detective Inspector."

Riley visibly shrank into the back of the mill as Ant's temper reached a crescendo. Absolute silence fell. Only the freshening breeze broke the stillness as loose planks of the mill sides clattered against one another.

"Have you finished? Because I would like to go now." Susan's voice was calm, measured and assertive.

Her voice redirected Ant's thoughts back to the matter in hand. His temper had quickly subsided. He was once more focused on the job.

"Oh, I don't think so, Susan. Another few minutes should do, but I don't think it's home you will be going to for some time." He purposely threw the detective a cold stare. "Now, where were we? Oh yes, the running-away bit. You see, several seemingly different things came together to prove you killed Burt, some through luck, others by merely joining the dots.

The woman failed to react.

"As I said, you have been very clever. Even going to the extreme of tearing any personal details from letters you received, oh and forgetting to add your name or address to some little notes you wrote."

For the first time, Susan reacted. "What do you mean?"

"Do you like sailing, Susan?"

The woman shrugged her shoulders.

"Given the state of your boat, I'm assuming it's not the most favourite of your hobbies, but handy for nipping up and down the broad, isn't it? Especially when you can tuck it away up a side channel. It was only by chance that the river warden saw it. And if you had bothered to buy a river licence that would have been the end of it. That was your first mistake."

Susan's cheeks began to twitch.

Lyn's quiet voice floated across the mill. "Stan Fleming is nothing but thorough. He didn't give up in trying to trace the owner of the boat, did he, Fitch?"

Ant smiled with satisfaction as the late arrival said his piece.

"That's right, Lyn. I've just come from his place, and he confirmed he traced you. Seems you had your boat serviced this time last year to get it ready for the new season. Stan had a hunch there would be a service record somewhere, and it had to be local. Belling's Marine Services identified the boat from Stan's description. They were surprised it was still afloat given what they had to deal with when you brought it in."

Still, she gave nothing away.

"Then we come to the clincher, or rather—two. If only you had stood at the back of the group when Lyn took those pictures of you last Saturday. Who knows, you may never have come to our attention. As it is, Susan, the river warden recognised you as the person he saw weeks ago walking away from the boat. Jennifer's daughter, Sophie, also recognised you as the person who came around with a sympathy card.

He watched as Susan pulled a confused face.

"Oh, you didn't see her. But she saw you. She also watched you rifling through Burt's desk drawers when her mother was busy making you a drink. What were you looking for? It couldn't have been the note we found in the garage, could it? You really do have to be more polite when you write to people, and I'm sure your fingerprints will be all over it."

Susan slumped in her chair; her eyes fixed firmly on Ant.

"But what about poor Albert?" asked Ron Busby.

Lyn responded, "I'm afraid Susan murdered him as well."

Once more, the room erupted, apart from Jennifer, who wept quietly in the corner, and Susan, who had yet to take her eyes off Ant.

"It took some doing, but the footage Ant's friend managed to enhance of Albert entering the church tower clearly shows a second person. One who wears shiny bracelets. Like the one you are wearing, Susan."

The woman diverted her attention from Ant for a split second as she glanced at the wrist band before returning her gaze to him.

Ron Busby screamed at Susan, "You are evil. Why Albert? He liked you?"

Ant cut in, "As I said earlier, the people who like this lady tend to get hurt. Now I don't know for sure. Perhaps we'll never know. But my hunch is that Susan lured him to the church. The vicar told me the key to the church steeple had been taken." Ant looked at the vicar, who was nodding his head, sadness etched across his face. "I suspect you told him what you had done and that, together, you could buy the mill inexpensively and live happily ever after. When he refused, you realised you needed to get rid of the only other person who knew you had murdered Burt Bampton. I'm told once you have killed once, it's easier the second time. Isn' t that right, Detective Inspector?"

It was all the bewildered policeman could do to nod his agreement.

"Just one question, Anthony. How did she kill my husband?"

The room once more fell silent as the stark honesty of Jennifer's question sank in.

"Lyn?"

She accepted Ant's invitation. "Unlucky for Susan I stumbled across her at a chemist a few days ago. I have to give it to you. You had me fooled with all those tears. Later I got to thinking about what Ant and I found out about Burt's illness. Diabetes needs watching. Too much sugar in the blood and the sufferer will have a hyper, or to be more precise, a hyperglycaemic attack. If the blood sugar falls too low, that's bad too and can lead to hypoglycaemia. Sounds almost the same, doesn't it, but they are not. Overprescribing the main medication for type-two diabetics, Metformin, will cause the sufferer's blood pressure to plummet, resulting in light-headedness and ultimately collapse, and worse if left untreated."

"But what has this got to do with anything, Miss Blackthorn?"

Lyn kept her cool, amused that Riley bothered to show at least a modicum of politeness.

"Because Burt recently ran out of his medication. I assume he must have lost some of his tablets. Now, a vital issue with diabetes is that regular medication is an absolute must. So what did Burt do? He was nearby where Susan worked, so he popped in for an emergency prescription. He recognised her from her previous contact wanting him to sell the mill to her but I imagine thought nothing of it; he just needed his tablets. Unluckily for Burt, she was in the shop on her own. Although it's against all medical protocol, she dispensed the Metformin. Jennifer, do you have them with you?"

The tearful widow stood and held an arm out.

"Now, those took some finding. Burt Bampton did all he could to hide his condition from Jennifer."

Lyn took the box of pills and looked at the printed instructions. She held the package aloft. "It says to take four 250 milligrams per day with food."

Lyn opened the box and slid out a sleeve of tablets. "The foil says these are five hundred milligram tablets. In effect, Susan increased the dose by a hundred per cent. Burt had only just started taking his medication. The information Ant and I came across was clear. He was being started on a low dose to see how he tolerated the drug. Burt had no chance once he took the prescription Susan dispensed. True, she didn't know what would happen or when. Unluckily for her, and Burt, he collapsed on a set of steep stairs and hit his head on the floor. By the time professional help arrived, it was too late."

Susan got to her feet and shrieked at Jennifer, "I told him the mill belonged to my family and was cheated out of it by his. We've tried for hundreds of years to get this place back, always prepared to pay a fair price even though it's ours by right. Would he listen? No. It didn't matter how much money I offered him; he still refused. I tried being nice, just like my ancestors, but where did it get us? Nowhere. Well if we can't have it, at least he hasn't got it anymore either."

By now, Jennifer was inconsolable. Neither the vicar's

nor Lyn's efforts could calm her. As Riley moved forward to take hold of the murderer, Ron Busby spoke up.

"And Albert?"

Susan Mylnweard smiled at him and shrugged her shoulders.

EPILOGUE

Bampton Mill stood silent once more. Riley had called for backup and removed Susan Mylnweard to the cells. The remainder of the invited guests had left, some more relieved than others. Only Riley, Fitch, Ant, and Lyn remained, though there was little conversation between them. Eventually, Detective Inspector Riley mumbled a few words.

"I suppose I should thank you three for tonight, though I have to say if you'd had been more open with me all along, we might have tied this thing up a lot sooner."

Ant seemed to sum up the feelings of the other two. "And if you could curb your tendency to think blue if we say red, or accident if we think murder, we might all get along a little better."

"And how do I know you lot will behave any differently than you have over the last few months?"

The stand off lasted just a few seconds before Fitch broke the impasse. "Perhaps, just perhaps, a good start might be for both of you to stop sniping at one another. You never know, it might just allow you to start trusting one another."

Riley curled his lip as Ant frowned at the policeman.

"Well, I'm prepared to give it a go if you are, Detective Inspector?" He glanced sideways at Lyn, who looked thoroughly sceptical.

"I tell you what, gentlemen, why don't I knock us up a light supper, and we find out a bit more about each other. Oh, and Detective, I'll even prepare a little something for the dog."

Mention of Riley's pet seemed to rouse the animal, which began to bark loudly.

The detective instinctively turned in the direction of the incessant noise. "Blow me, I forgot about him."

Fitch was onto it. "Stay there, I'll bring the beast in."

Seconds later an excited springer spaniel, its tail wagging furiously, strained at the leash to reach his master.

"Oh, I almost forgot, talking about food, we have something for you, Inspector." Ant strolled over to a wall cupboard and took a tubular package from the top shelf. "Lyn and I felt for you when we came to see you. We thought you could do with your own secret supply of chocolate digestives that you could keep away from your superior."

Riley's eyes widened as he slipped the treat out of a paper bag.

Heavens, I think he's going to cry.

Ant need not have worried; the detective soon regained control of his emotions as he held the packet as if it were a bar of gold. Unfortunately for him, the sight of food tipped his dog into a frenzy, enabling him to slip his leash, jump up to steal the package and run out of the mill.

Riley's face dropped as the others began to laugh.

"Come here with my biscuits, Igor, before I..."

The remainder of his threats were lost to the others as the policeman ran from the mill clutching an empty paper bag in one hand and an old police whistle in the other.

END

ENGLISH (UK) TO US ENGLISH GLOSSARY

- **Biggles:** Fictional British WWI ace fighter pilot
- **Bin:** Trash can
- **Biscuit:** Cookies
- **Blues & Twos:** Flashing lights on an emergency vehicle
- **Boffins: UK:** Slang word much used in both world wars used to describe scientists and other highly educated people undertaking secret work. Has connotations of being eccentric as in "looked like a mad scientist"
- **Boiled sweet:** Candy mainly made from sugar and flavourings boiled into a hard treat
- **Bonnet:** (car) Hood
- **Broad:** A stretch of shallow water formed from old peat diggings. Common in Norfolk and Suffolk regions of the UK. Can take the form of narrow stretches of water, like canals, or open water, like small lakes.
- **Buttercross:** A type of market associated with

English market towns and dating from medieval times.

- **Car boot:** Trunk
- **Car-Boot Sale:** Garage sale that takes place at a venue with many other sellers
- **Chunter:** To talk or grumble monotonously
- **Cruddy:** Dirty. "His boots were cruddy."
- **Cock** (of the school): Recognised by his or her school peers as the toughest/best fighter
- **Dicky:** Traditional slang for upset: "My stomach is a bit dicky."
- **Dixon of Dock Green:** Famous TV Police character (sergeant) in series that ran from 1955 to 1976
- **Estate Agent:** Realtor
- **Full English:** Short form for "a full English breakfast"
- **GCHQ:** Acronym for British Secret Service Headquarters in London
- **Jib Door:** A door decorated/panelled to look identical to the decoration of the wall in which it is placed.
- **Load of Old Tosh:** To talk rubbish/nonsense
- **Lord Chamberlain:** The most senior administrative post holder in the royal household to the Monarch
- **Maltesers:** A candy consisting a light, crunchy malt ball centre covered in milk chocolate.
- **Mini-Van:** MPV
- **MoT:** Acronym for "Ministry of Transport" - refers to mandatory annual road worthiness check

- **Nesh**: lack of hardiness, "It's not cold; you're just nesh.'"
- **Nick**: To steal something
- **Not on Your Nelly**: British rhyming slang for "life" - Not on your Nelly Duff = Puff = Life
- **Nowt**: North of England dialect for "nothing"
- **Ofsted**: Acronym for education inspection body (Office for Standards in Education)
- **On the Wonk**: Out of level: "That shelf is on the wonk."
- **Pear Drop**: Traditional UK boiled candy
- **Plaster**: Band-Aids
- **Rafty**: Norfolk dialect for damp or raw (cold/windy) weather
- **Rich Tea**: A type of sweet biscuit; the ingredients generally include wheat flour, sugar, vegetable oil and malt extract
- **Sarky**: Short form of the word sarcastic
- **Screaming Abdabs**: To induce an attack of extreme anxiety or irritation
- **Shufti**: To reconnoitre: "Let's have a quick shufti at the house."
- **Skip**: Dumpster
- **Skiving**: Avoiding work, school or task: to shirk one's duties
- **Sums**: Math
- **Soft Lad**: Liverpool friendly slang for a fool
- **Staith**: A Norfolk term for a landing stage to load/unload goods from
- **Swan about**: Slang word meaning to be lazy, "I worked hard while you lot were swanning about."
- **Taking the Mick**: Slang for making fun of someone

- **Thruppence:** A UK coin used until 1971 and worth approximately one US cent today
- **Tip up:** Slang term meaning to arrive unannounced
- **Toff:** Slang word for upper class or rich person generally seen to be "looking down" on other people
- **Wherry:** A traditional sailboat used for carrying goods and passengers on the Norfolk & Suffolk Broads
- **Windscreen:** Car windshield

DID YOU ENJOY MILLER'S END?

Reviews are so important in helping get my books noticed. Unlike the big, established authors and publishers, I don't have the resources available for big marketing campaigns and expensive book launches (though I live in hope!)

What I *do* have, gratefully, is the following of a loyal and growing band of readers.

Genuine reviews of my writing help bring my books to the attention of new readers.

If you enjoyed this book, it would be a great help if you could spare a couple of minutes and kindly head over to my Amazon page to leave a review (as short or long as you like). All you need do is click on one of the links below.

- UK
- US

Thank you so much.

JOIN MY READERS' CLUB

Getting to know my readers is the thing I like most about writing. From time to time I publish a newsletter with details on my new releases, special offers, and other bits of news relating to the Norfolk Murder Mystery series. If you join my Readers' Club, I'll send you this gripping short story free and ONLY available to club members:

A Record of Deceit

Grace Pinfold is terrified a stranger wants to kill her. Disturbing phone calls and mysterious letters confirm the threat is real. Then Grace disappears. Ant and Lyn fear they have less than forty-eight hours to find Grace before tragedy strikes, a situation made worse by a disinterested Detective Inspector Riley who's convinced an innocent explanation exists.

Character Backgrounds

Read fascinating interviews with the four lead characters in the Norfolk Cozy Mysteries series. Anthony Stanton, Lyn Blackthorn, Detective Inspector Riley, and Fitch explain what drives them, their backgrounds, and let slip an insight into each of their characters. We also learn how Ant, Lyn, and Fitch first met as children and grew up to be firm friends even if they do drive each other crazy most of the time!

You can get your free content by visiting my website at www.keithjfinney.com

I look forward to seeing you there.

Keith

For Joan, who is always there for me.

ACKNOWLEDGMENTS

Cover design by Books Covered

Line Edit: Paula. paulaproofreader.wixsite.com/home

Proof Reader: Terrance Grundy of Editerry

ALSO BY KEITH FINNEY

In the Norfolk Murder Mystery Series:

Dead Man's Trench

Narky Collins, Stanton Parva's most hated resident, lies dead at the bottom of an excavation trench. Was it an accident, or murder?

Amateur sleuths, Ant and Lyn, team up to untangle a jumble of leads as they try to discover the truth when jealousy, greed, and blackmail combine in an explosive mix of lies and betrayal.

Will the investigative duo succeed, or fall foul of Detective Inspector Riley?

Murder by Hanging

Ethan Baldwin hangs from a tree in woods just outside the quiet Norfolk village of Stanton Parva. The police think the respected church warden committed suicide. **Ant and Lyn are certain someone murdered Ethan and set out to bring his ruthless killer to justice.**

Suspects include a greedy land developer, a vicar in turmoil, and a businessman about to lose everything.

Can our amateur sleuths solve the crime, or will the killer get away scot-free?

The Boathouse Killer

Successful businessman, Geoff Singleton, is found dead in the cabin of his cruiser on the Norfolk Broads. His wife's ex-partner suddenly appears, and a secret which someone does not want exposed merge into a countdown to catastrophe.

When the body of a respected young entrepreneur is discovered, sat bolt upright with unseeing eyes, Detective Inspector Riley concludes it's a heart attack.

Ant and Lyn are suspicious; why would a fit man suddenly die? *The deeper they dig, the more the inconsistencies mount.* Convinced the police are wrong, the pair have just days to identify the killer before DI Riley turns on them with the threat of arrest for perverting the course of justice. *Will the killer be exposed? Or will their evil scheming pay off?*

www.keithjfinney.com

FACEBOOK

NOTICES

PUBLISHED BY:
Norfolk Cozy Mystery Publishing
Copyright © 2020

www.keithjfinney.com

Printed in Great Britain
by Amazon

23676147R00128